ROMA

THE

INVENTOR

A SUPERNATURAL SOCIETY
NOVELLA

ROMANCING THE INVENTOR

A SUPERNATURAL SOCIETY NOVELLA

GAIL CARRIGER

GAIL CARRIGER LLC

GAIL CARRIGER, LLC

Copyright © 2016 by GAIL CARRIGER, LLC
Reprint 2018

Cover photo © Donna Ricci. All rights reserved.
Photo by Pixie Vision Photography
Cover © 2016 by Gail Carriger, LLC,
assembled by Starla Huchton
Formatting by Nina Pierce of Seaside Publications

ISBN 978-1-944751-07-4

ACKNOWLEDGEMENTS

Flirt, a little poem for you...
Lost love well spent
on the ending we didn't get.
~ Fiendish

A Note on Chronology

The Supernatural Society Novellas can be read in any order.

This particular story is set in the summer of 1878. It is thus two years after the final Parasol Protectorate book, *Timeless*. Genevieve Lefoux was first introduced to readers in *Changeless*. She also appears as a child, Vieve, in the Finishing School series. However, this novella can be enjoyed without having read any of Gail's other works. Although it's always fun to play a rousing game of "spot that side character."

CHAPTER ONE

In Which We Hope Werewolves are Perverted

Summer 1878

"I've taken work at the big house." Imogene spoke into the awkward silence at the end of supper. They needed to know now, because she started that very night.

Her mother looked up, exhaustion inked around eyes bright with horror. "No. Imogene, please, no. Not you. They'll take you for a drone, try to keep you forever."

"Really, Ma. Why should they? I've no artistic talent to speak of. No painting, nor pottery, nor pickling, nor what have you. I'll be perfectly fine. It's not even an indenture, simply good honest work, lighter than the fields, easier than the farm. You know how handy I am with a duster. Tall enough to reach all the difficult spots." The fact that they desperately needed the money hung in the air, unsaid.

Ma ignored both the said and the unsaid. Ignored the hunger still present at the table, though the littles had eaten all that was there. "You want a good position? Marry."

Imogene raised her eyebrows. "Positioning me on my back, yet still dusting? You're too kind."

"Don't be smart with me. That beauty of yours won't last forever, my girl. The butcher was asking after you only this morning. He's still hopeful and he's got a good business." Mrs Hale flapped a work-red hand – a weak attempt to physically dismiss her eldest daughter's disgust.

"The butcher cheats his customers." *Now, if his sister offered...* Imogene knew Mr Bouchard's cheating for a fact because she could do complex sums in her head and had caught him in the act. Even though she'd been distracted by Miss Bouchard at the time. Mary had the most luscious lips. Probably something to do with access to all that meat.

"Haw, look at you, high and mighty, so wise with the numbers."

Imogene sniffed.

"So, he cheats. All tradesmen cheat. Yes, I know, he ain't half good enough for you. None of them ever are."

Imogene closed her eyes, using exasperation to hide fear. Let her mother think her haughty. Let the men of the village think her rejections stemmed from arrogance. It was so much safer that way. "Exactly. I prefer dusters. They're so pleasingly feathery and round, and they can be twirled. No man in this village would abide a twirling."

Mrs Hale lowered her voice. Much good it did; the littles were all ears. "Be serious, Imogene, you can't go. Them's *perverted* at the big house."

Precisely the appeal, Imogene thought but didn't say. Maybe they would know what was wrong with her. Maybe they could fix her. Or guide her. Could never tell Ma *that* reason for going into service.

"They may not want a poor country lass for fangs, even one with your looks, but they'll likely want something else from you. It ain't worth the risk. You'll spoil your prospects. Such as they are, you having refused every eligible bachelor for leagues and getting long in the tooth besides."

Imogene's reply was to twist the subject. "You'd prefer we had the werewolves back? At least the vampires bring in extra work. Plus, they don't come crashing through town every ripe moon." She hid a smile at the idea of vampires crashing anything, aside from a carriage and four.

But Ma was in one of her moods. "At least you could've leashed one of *them*. Werewolves marry. Vampires don't."

Imogene jerked her chin up. This was partly why everyone thought her prideful, her response was all too often an up-tilted nose coupled with sullen silence. *There goes Imogene Hale, thinks she's better than us. Thinks the world owes her more than a pretty face and fine figure.*

Imogene didn't care because that way, they never guessed the truth behind the up-tilt. She'd rather be thought mean than bent.

The werewolves had guessed.

Well, one of them had. Not so much guessed as known straight up. An odd encounter. She'd been out after dark, not a custom for a single girl, but Ma'd had one of her spells and Imogene had trekked across town after a tincture of willow bark. She'd noticed more shadows than usual at the pub. Big shadows. The pack had returned from abroad and was out for a drink with fellow soldiers. One of them hadn't been interested in ale. He'd been looking to flirt and caught her in his claws.

"Beautiful lady, where are you going so quickly?" He'd moved very fast to block her path.

She'd looked on him; hard not to with a man that big. Taller than Imogene by a hand or more, and she was no sprout. He was easy on the eyes, no doubting that, like moonlight brought to life. He knew it too. He treasured it as part of his character, keeping it front-facing when he spoke – words behind his words. *Look at me – ain't I the living end?* Or perhaps it only came off that way, like her beauty. Such icy eyes. She'd wondered what *his* secret was, the one that made his chin up-tilt in arrogance. Was it as dire as hers?

She knew very well what made him stare. A girl too delicate for common blood, even with the muscles of hard labor layered over her tall frame, skin too smooth and clear, hair too dark and glossy. Imogene's slender beauty was all court lady and little country lass, adding to her aura of arrogance. She'd eyes too big not to be bold and a mouth too lush to hold its peace. Imogene was allure damped by poverty, but not snuffed out. He'd looked at her and taken in all the things that made the village men come offering. Only he'd likely ask for more. Or maybe he'd steal it. *Gentleman* and *werewolf* made for uneasy bedfellows; sometimes *werewolf* came out on top.

She hadn't been afraid. Not really. *Gentleman* usually won with a Woolsey Pack member, or the Alpha would hear of it and tear throats. Lord Maccon's werewolves didn't savage their neighborhood's goodwill.

But Imogene hadn't reacted rightly to his beauty. She hadn't really registered it except aesthetically. He'd noticed *that*.

"Beautiful lady," he'd repeated. "But not at all inclined. Pity."

He'd leaned in a little, not so close as to be rude, but certainly enough to make the hearts of most maidens flutter. Except hers. *I'm flawed,* she'd thought, analyzing how handsome he was.

"What is it, my sweet little thing? Broken heart? Can't be that you've given it away – even the married ones react to me."

Very arrogant, then. "How do you know I have a heart?"

"She speaks."

Imogene didn't say anything more, merely looked into his eyes. Direct. A maiden was supposed to lower her lashes before any man, let alone a gentleman soldier. But a werewolf took careful handling.

He'd stared back. Searching for something and, finally, finding it. "Ah, so. No. Utterly uninterested in a man, I think. Or is it men in general?"

Imogene had never felt more exposed than at that moment. No one had ever spoken her secret aloud. She'd lowered her lashes and whispered, so softly only his supernatural ears could hear, "Please, m'lord. Don't tell."

The werewolf had only sighed. "What a waste. No, don't be ashamed. What do I care? Who would I tell? And why bother? I don't even know your name to speak it. It's not as if you had a choice, after all." Then he'd *tsk*ed. "Poor child. The countryside is no place for a tom."

With which enigmatic statement he'd twisted out of her path and, executing a mocking little bow, let her on her way.

Imogene hurried off. Her skin prickled with exposure, as if his knowing words had needled her, inside and out, sewing her with the threads of his understanding. Visible stitches. What one werewolf knew, the whole pack knew.

But they'd kept her secret, and now they were gone.

And vampires were perverted.

Or so she hoped.

Vampires were indeed perverted, as it turned out.

But it didn't do Imogene any good.

She was hired on after only the briefest of interviews with one of the drones. She didn't know whether to be flattered or insulted. It was true, vampires always needed new blood, but she'd like to think they saw some value in her besides the veins of her shapely white neck.

Woolsey Castle's previous occupants, the werewolf pack, had lived sparingly in the sprawling manor. They'd keep assorted clavigers as valets, one capable butler, and a few footmen and groundskeepers, but that was all they required in the way of domestics.

Vampires, on the other hand, lived in high style. They insisted on everything being perfect and perfectly spotless. They had drones for food and entertainment, just as werewolves had clavigers, but nowhere near enough. And, of course, drones wouldn't deign to undertake menial tasks. In addition, the hive entertained a constant stream of guests, several artists in residence, and one very demanding canine (a Papillon puppy named Skootnaughtel, or Skoot for short). All of these kept odd hours and needed the attendance of an army of staff (particularly Skoot). The fact that the vampires occasionally referred to their servants as *nibbles* was neither here nor there.

Imogene intended to become one of those snacks.

It started out well; the hive appreciated beauty. This kept Imogene out of the kitchens and put her amongst the upstairs staff – where she could be displayed to advantage. Too old for chambermaid and too crass for lady's maid, parlourmaid seemed the natural choice. She was given a crisp black dress and a starched white pinafore to wear over it, in the French style; these emphasized her fine bone structure and gentle curves. She was instructed to pull her dark hair back but to keep it soft about her face. By the end of the first week, she'd proved herself quite handy with a duster, which landed her the daytime rotation. This suited her well enough, except it afforded her little opportunity to research vampire perversions.

She became friendly with Skoot, who, in personality, form, and frivolity, rather resembled her favorite duster.

"It's easy work," she told her mother on her trip home for seven-day. "I share a room with one of the upstairs maids, but she works nights, so I mostly have it to myself."

"And your mistress and masters, they are kind?"

"I rarely see the vampires, Ma, my duties are during daylight hours. I like it. The visitors are varied and mostly absentminded geniuses."

Mrs Hale shook her head. "I don't know about you being exposed to such characters. It's not right for an innocent young girl."

"I'm not so young anymore."

"But still innocent. Or I'll know the reason why."

"Yes, Ma."

Except that Imogene wished to be decidedly less innocent. She'd found the courage to approach the hive, but she was no closer to exploring her own perversions. She'd thought being exposed to vampires would help her understand why, for as long as she could remember, she'd never looked to a man. Oh, she noticed them, she interacted with them (they were, after all, *people*), but when the other girls of the village started to flirt, and the men flirted back, it was without her. Imogene had watched the girls. She'd always watched the girls. The soft swell of cheek, and notch of vulnerability at the base of the neck. Smooth curves and sweet smiles, glossy hair and soft skin – why want anything else? So, she'd avoided both, and they thought her arrogant.

Even young, she'd realized it wasn't normal. *She* wasn't normal. As she got older, she'd understood that it also wasn't legal. Supernaturals were the exception. But supernaturals were the exception to *everything*. And they were mostly men.

So, she'd stuffed it away in fear. Until the vampires came, because inside a hive (as everyone knows), things were different. Inside a hive, the vampire queen had absolute authority. She protected her people, except from herself.

Imogene had hoped, perhaps, that she'd catch the countess's full attention. Hoped in vain (or should that be vein?), as it transpired.

It started well. "You are quite the prettiest creature, aren't you?" Countess Nadasdy said when Imogene was finally brought before her a month into her employment. "So long as you can string a sentence together, you'll do nicely."

Imogene wasn't entirely sure what she expected. Aside from neck nibbles, of course. The queen was attractive, in a sweetly rounded, tavern-wench kind of way. *Curves are good. Perhaps she'll dismiss the other vampires and ravish me? Maybe neck bites will turn to kisses?* Imogene had never kissed anyone, not willingly. Not a girl. And by heaven, she wanted to. More than kisses too. Although she'd no idea what that might entail. *But I'm a quick study.*

The queen turned away to one of her male vampires. "I wager she tastes as sweet as she looks, Ambrose."

Imogene held her breath in giddy anticipation and fear.

Ambrose regarded Imogene down his nose. "I'd be careful with country meat, my queen, it can be quite tough."

"Surely not one as fine as this?"

"Look at the eyes, my queen." That was one of the other vampires, Dr Caedes.

Countess Nadasdy gave a gesture and someone pushed Imogene forward. Imogene stumbled, righted herself, and marched directly to the queen. Up-tilt in place.

The other vampires present tensed as she neared Countess Nadasdy.

Imogene lowered her eyes and curtsied, offering her neck.

"She hasn't been vetted for intimate contact!" objected Lord Ambrose.

"Pish tosh," said the queen. "Now look at me, child."

Imogene looked. The countess had freckles on her nose. It was unexpected and vampirically question-able. Of course, they could be fake. Imogene started to count them. Counting made her feel less frightened.

The countess placed a cool hand beneath her chin. "I see what you mean, Caedes. Willful."

The vampire's skin was very white. The tips of her fangs poked out slightly as she parted her lips in concentration.

Imogene shivered. *Twenty-six, twenty-seven…*

"To break or to bend, do you think?"

Imogene thought the countess lovely. She looked as much like a country lass as Imogene herself looked like an aristocratic countess. *Thirty, thirty-one…*

"Either one might be fun. Unless you think her better left preserved." Dr Caedes was a cautious man.

Now I'm a jar of jam, thought Imogene.

"Wait? Surely not." Apparently, the queen objected to Imogene-flavored jam.

"I've an idea she might be best left to mature, like a fine wine. A certain eagerness may result." The doctor was a peculiar vampire, tall and skinny as a deer midwinter, with thinning hair. Imogene hadn't thought they made ugly vampires.

Lord Ambrose was sitting back now, watching the proceedings with ill-disguised contempt. "What rot. One doesn't rest country ale. It goes sour."

Imogene winced, offended.

Countess Nadasdy's eyes narrowed. "No, I believe I see your point, Caedes. We wait."

Thus, the hive agreed to forget about Imogene.

And forget her they did. She was never summoned to the queen's chambers like some of the other maids (and all of the footmen). She was never even asked to serve Countess Nadasdy at supper.

At first this was frustrating. *I should like to be corrupted! What else are vampires good for?* But after another month's employment, Imogene decided this might be a good thing.

Countess Nadasdy proved too cruel. She cared

not for maids' feelings on the matter of sharing her chamber. Imogene roomed with a frail blonde, fine-boned and rosy-cheeked. A night chambermaid, she sported bruises and lacerations every week after visiting the queen. The collar of her housedress became ever higher. She returned to the room clutching boiled sweets and fresh oranges from foreign lands. She added a new shawl to her tiny wardrobe, silk paisley from Paris, far too fine for a maid. But Imogene caught her crying over that shawl. They were not friends, so she couldn't ask: did she weep because of the bruises, or the bites, or some other thing a vampire queen could make a girl feel?

Imogene envied her. Not the bites, or the bruises, or the sweets, or even the shawl for that matter. Although it was *very* pretty. No, she envied her the experience, and the attention.

Not that the queen remained constant. She kept mostly male drones, and they received the lion's share of her attention. She would drop quickly any member of staff in favor of a new toy. For drones were vastly superior to maids – famous sculptors and portrait artists, even one renowned classical composer. They filled Woolsey Castle with music and art, drifting about in a fog of intellectualism, and like any fog, they were unpredictable and occasionally quite damp.

Imogene was never summoned. Forgotten in the daylight, going about her duties with a quiet competence and a particularly fluffy feather duster, she felt as if she were sleepwalking. *Apparently, even here there is something wrong with me. Some reason the queen ignores me.* Thankfully, the male vampires also seemed to have forgotten her. She was not so foolish as to think they, like her long-ago werewolf suitor, would honor her preferences. Vampires were not werewolves. Everyone knew the truth – werewolves were the real gentlemen, vampires only *acted* like gentlemen.

Rejected though she might feel and sometimes quite lonely, the hive was still better than the village. No one had asked for her hand in months. Much as she loved her brothers and sisters, it was nice to share a room with only one other person. And the pay was good. When she made it home, Ma looked a little less tired and the littles a little less hungry.

"Take this out to the lab, Imogene, do." Henry, the daytime first footman, pressed a tray into her hands and gestured at the back door.

"Pardon me?" Imogene was a member of the *upper* household, and upstairs staff did *not* go outside during working hours!

"The potting shed, down the path there? You must know it."

"Leave the house?" Imogene remained dumbfounded.

"Well, yes, technically. Although I believe they consider the shed a part of the hive – rather an important part. Drone Lefoux is back. The bell just went, demanding tea."

Imogene blinked. "Who?"

Henry slapped his forehead. "Of course, you were taken on *after* the young master left for university. Drone Lefoux, you know? Not technically a *true* drone but belongs to the hive, one of our queen's most valued indentures. Best one, if you ask me. Punishment from the crown and our considerable gain. Lefoux, the famous inventor? Come, come, you must know the name."

Imogene only blinked. "No."

"Haven't you read a paper in the last few years?" Henry was an educated man, lucky sod.

Imogene gave a wide-eyed look of utter confusion. "I can't read. What do you take me for, gentry?"

"You're so good with numbers, I forgot." Henry had put Imogene to work counting the silver the moment he learned of her odd talent with sums.

Imogene smiled at him. "Born with that, I'm afraid. No schooling."

Henry blinked at the smile, dazed, then shook it off. "Four years ago, the gossip was all over town. A monstrous metal octopus on the rampage?"

Imogene only continued to shake her head, feeling ever more confused. As if London gossip held any sway in village life.

"Well, Drone Lefoux is famous. Possibly a little evil and definitely resentful of being forced into exile in the countryside, but always doing something interesting in that laboratory. That laboratory being the *potting shed*, if you take my meaning. You should be thrilled to take out the tea. Now go on, do, before it gets cold."

Intrigued, Imogene did as ordered.

Imogene knocked, several times, getting progressively louder. There was a considerable racket coming from the other side of the door, and whoever was inside couldn't possibly have heard her. So, she pushed it open herself, balancing the tray on one hip.

Inside, the shed seemed bigger than Imogene initially thought. And louder, full of hisses and bangs and the scent of hot oil and smoke. It was lined with shelves that were stuffed to bursting. There were stacks of engines and engine parts, some of which seemed to be moving. The air was thick with steam and smoke. There were coils and tubes, bottles of odd-colored liquids and any number of tools, some quite rude-looking. *That one looks like a... never mind.* Every available surface was littered with curiosities; larger implements were propped up against walls or hanging from the ceiling. A coil of glass tubing snaked around the crown molding, filled with a bubbling orange gas that lit the interior with an eerie artificial glow. Perched in one corner, like some sort of ship's figurehead, was an oddly sinister wicker chicken. It frowned down upon her with an air of chubby disdain.

Imogene wasn't sure she liked being judged by a chicken.

The only focal point in the chaos was a desk in the far corner, strewn with stacks of papers which turned out (to Imogene's delight) to be sketches and annotated schematics (rather than lines of incomprehensible script). *Concepts for more machines!* She would have loved to page through them, but her hands were full, and that would certainly be considered prying.

Next to the desk was a massive piece of flat river slate, mounted on the wall; someone was using it to make calculations with chalk. Imogene might not have her letters, but she could read numbers *and* do complex sums. Or she'd thought they were complex, multiplication and division and all sorts that left her ma in awe and the littles confused. But the sums written on that slate also included letters, making them more mysterious and more intriguing than anything she'd ever seen before.

Imogene was studying it with her head cocked, holding the tea, and wondering where to put the tray, when a figure emerged out of the chaos.

A slender man straightened up from where he'd been crouched under one of the larger contraptions. He wore protective goggles, some kind of helmet, and large leather gloves. Good thing too, for sparks were flying from a heating tube he held in one hand. An arc of blue shot up from beneath his ministrations, casting purple sparks everywhere.

Imogene nearly dropped the tea tray.

The man swore loudly, either because of the sparks or because one cuff was on fire. He slapped at his sleeve absently, so it wasn't that.

Finally, the man put down the tube, muttering in a slippery sort of foreign language.

Imogene took the momentary lull as an opportunity to say, "Sir? I've brought your tea."

The man jumped and dropped the tube, which began hissing. He cursed roundly, then jerked back as an arc of purple flew up to the ceiling.

He whirled, charging at Imogene in a sudden sprint. He grabbed her by the waist and pulled her (still balancing the tray) behind a large metal something that, if pressed, Imogene would have called a fish tank.

Behind them came a loud bang and an even louder crash.

The man yanked off his goggles and helmet in a smooth movement and cast them carelessly to one side. This revealed a sweet pixie face framed by short, dark, wavy hair.

"What the hell do you think you're doing?"

Imogene could only stare.

He, as it turned out, was a she.

CHAPTER TWO

In Which Inventors Have Powerful Dimples

Imogene swallowed, throat dry, and wished the tea was hers. She needed fortification. The shed was hotter and more cramped than she'd initially thought. The woman's face was smudged by a thin line of soot across one sharp cheekbone.

The *woman*, without a doubt that's what the inventor actually was. She contented herself with pulling off her large leather gloves and ranting. "You have ruined *days* of work. I nearly had it calibrated perfectly. Now I shall have to start over. And there is a good chance the explosion took out my notes."

There was a hint of a foreign accent to her words. It made them sound silky. The inventor was wearing men's clothing under a workman's leather apron, and as Imogene watched she actually unbuttoned the cuffs (one burnt) and began rolling *up* her sleeves!

"Well, don't just stand there, girl. You can speak, can you not?" At which juncture the inventor – *What had Henry said her name was? Oh yes, Lefoux –* finally turned from the carnage in her laboratory to look Imogene full in the face.

"I was told to bring your tea," said Imogene, inanely, feeling all at once self-conscious and guilty and frustrated. *I didn't mean to mess up the experiment. I was only doing as ordered.*

She tried a hesitant smile.

Drone Lefoux stared at her for a long moment, blinking in a sort of trance. Perhaps she'd caught some of the blast? Her eye color was hard to see in the dingy interior, but Imogene thought they might be green.

Then the inventor smiled back.

She has dimples. I love dimples. Oh, dear.

"I did ask for tea, didn't I? Where's Henry? He knows my foibles, and not to come inside at a delicate time. I'd sooner cold tea than a failed experiment."

"He gave me the tray." A statement, if possible, even more inane.

"Did he? Well, you should put it down, no?"

Imogene looked about, helpless. This part of the laboratory was a *little* cleaner than the rest, but there was still no free spot on any flat surface large enough to set a teacup, let alone a tea tray.

The inventor snorted. "Ah, I see. The desk will do. Don't mind the papers. A few drips will not hurt them – they have been through worse."

Imogene did as instructed, feeling awed and tongue-tied and clumsy. *How does such a glorious woman look so good as a man?*

She mustered up some courage. "I apologize. I

shan't make the mistake again. If I'm allowed back, what should I know to do better?"

The inventor was regarding her with newly focused interest, and sipping tea. She was still smiling.

Oh, please stop with the dimples. They burn.

Fortunately, Drone Lefoux couldn't smile and explain at the same time. "Knock as loudly as possible. If I do not answer, open the door and yell. Do not come in, wait a bit and yell again. It may take me a few moments to realize someone is here. And if the yelling does not work, the fresh air and sunlight often catches my attention."

Imogene regarded the pert face before her. The cheek smudge was, frankly, adorable, but the skin underneath was almost as pale as a vampire's. And those (maybe) green eyes looked tired. Did she take proper care of herself?

Before she could stop herself, Imogene said, "You don't need a break for a bit of air, do you? It can't be healthy to stay trapped indoors breathing *this* all of the time." Her gesture indicated the general aura of smoke and steam.

The dimples reappeared.

Imogene wondered if she could develop an immunity. Since she was now fantasizing about kissing them, probably not.

At least the inventor didn't find her concern officious.

"What a good idea! Let me finish my tea and we shall take a walk in the garden together."

Imogene blinked at her. "We shall?"

The inventor tilted her head. Her movements seemed always to be quick but not birdlike, more fluid. "You object to my company?"

"I do have other duties, ma'am."

"Madame, if you would."

Imogene felt a wave of crushing disappointment. She wasn't so ignorant of other cultures. She knew what the word *madame* meant in French. *She's married.*

"Madame. I should get back."

"Nonsense. Henry knows my ways. Tell him I needed your assistance with some task. I like to get to know new staff." The inventor finished her tea and stripped off her leather apron.

Underneath she had on grey trousers and a grey vest over a shirt that might once have been white. She wore no cravat or points, and the top button was open to show her throat. Imogene stared too long at that spot. Henry had said Lefoux was an indenture, not a real drone. That only meant she wasn't a *regular* food source. Imogene tried to see if there were any bite marks. She could still be lover to one of the vampires. But married?

Hanging the apron over a steam pipe, the inventor gave a little bow and offered Imogene her arm, as though she were a gentleman and Imogene a lady of quality.

Imogene took it, hands trembling slightly. She must look so very silly, in her servant's garb on the arm of such an important person.

"You are a dour little thing, no?" The inventor escorted her out into the back garden. She was taller than Imogene and leaner. Imogene relished the differences, collecting each new detail, adding them together into the perfect sum of temptation. Madame Lefoux was all angles, but graceful with them, confident in her movements and her address. Her nearness was exhilarating in a way Imogene had never felt before. And her eyes were indeed green, which, combined with the dimples, was entirely unfair of the universe.

Imogene said, pleased her voice remained steady, "This is an unexpected turn for my day, you must understand, Madame. I'm honored but confused."

The inventor gave her a sidelong look. "Yet you tolerate it with equanimity."

Imogene didn't know what the word *equanimity* meant, but she took it as a compliment. "There are often peculiar things at this house, Madame. I have learned to keep my own counsel." Although, of course, that was a skill she'd developed long before taking service.

"So, a Frenchwoman dressed as a man and taking you for a walk is not so out of the ordinary in a vampire house?"

Imogene inclined her head, looking up through long lashes.

The inventor said, as though the words were torn from her without will, "You are remarkably beautiful. I can see why the countess collected you." Then she winced. She paused their walk, arm tense under Imogene's sweaty hand. "May I?"

Imogene nodded, not understanding the request. But Madame Lefoux could do anything she wanted, because... dimples.

A tentative touch at Imogene's neck and the inventor's fingers pushed the high maid's collar down. Her green eyes were intent. Imogene's throat felt stretched and shivery.

"She has not claimed you? Or is it...? One of the males, then, for a different... use?" Madame Lefoux's lips twisted and she drew back her hand. "How long have you been employed here, Miss... I do not even know your name."

"Imogene, Madame. I'm only a parlourmaid." Her neck felt abandoned.

"I have never understood the English convention of disrespecting the working classes."

Imogene blushed with pleasure. "Miss Hale, then, if you prefer."

"I prefer it for now. Perhaps we will come back to Imogene eventually. I should have to earn the informality, though. Don't you feel?"

Imogene had never given it much thought. Servants were called by their given names – it was the way the world worked. "If I may do the same," she barely had the courage to whisper.

"Naturally." The inventor turned and they began to walk again.

Imogene was mortified that her hand was damp on the woman's arm, to be felt even under the rolled shirt at her elbow. The inventor's exposed wrists were bony, but sinewy and strong.

"And the other?" the inventor pressed her advantage.

Imogene blushed again, only this time with

shame. "I must surmise that they do not want me for that."

"What, *none* of them? Not even an introductory nibble?"

"Not a one."

"Are they *blind*?"

Imogene blushed all the harder. Whatever flaw the vampires saw in her, now this amazing woman would see it too. *I should be honored to have had a moment of her regard. Me, a parlourmaid, walking out with an intellectual giant. Not that it means anything.* No doubt the inventor was kind to all her subordinates. It would explain Henry's affection.

She confessed, "They made some comment at the beginning, but then I was given the day shift."

The inventor frowned. "Why on earth would they rusticate you? Have they forgotten about you or are they saving you for something?"

"I am to be preserved."

"Like smoked meat?"

"Your guess is likely better than mine, Madame."

They paused at the end of the garden before a wide lake that formed a natural barrier to the fields beyond.

The inventor lowered her arm.

Imogene dropped her hand quickly. No doubt Madame Lefoux would now reject her, as the vampires had, for some supposed willfulness in her eyes, seeing under the beauty to something flawed and warped.

Imogene tilted her nose slightly up, stared at the field, and waited to be rendered unworthy.

Callused fingers touched her chin, guiding her to look into green eyes. An unconscious mirroring of her first meeting with Countess Nadasdy, when the vampire queen had looked at Imogene and found her wanting.

The inventor did the same. "Poor lovely girl, you see it as rejection? You fancy yourself in love with one of them, then? Lord Ambrose, perhaps? He always catches the young ladies' eyes. Count yourself lucky, *choupinette*, they are not kind masters once they have you in their thrall. That you have survived this long unsullied is a miracle. Or very dangerous indeed."

Abruptly, she dropped her hand and turned her back on the lake. Offering her other arm. Imogene took it. Her chin tingled with the memory of that brief touch. It hadn't tingled with Countess Nadasdy, perhaps because the vampire's hand had been so soft. And so *very* cold.

Imogene wanted to brush aside the collar of Madame Lefoux's shirt to look for punctures. Did the inventor speak from personal experience? She scrambled for something to say. She wanted to ask about the husband that made the inventor a *madame*. But that would be presumptuous.

Henry had called Drone Lefoux the most valuable of the hive's indentures. Yet she was no real drone to serve every whim of her vampire masters and mistress. This meant the inventor owed the vampires her labor, but not her allegiance. How had that come about? Likely also an intrusive question. One did not ask a superior about business matters.

Her work, perhaps, is a safe topic? Tentatively, Imogene broke the silence. "On your slate, Madame, with the chalk… Why are there letters mixed in with the numbers?"

"Calculations for this counterstate aetheric conductor I am devising. It is giving me some trouble. You know algebra?"

Imogene shook her head.

"No, of course not. No university for parlourmaids, I suppose." The dimples took the sting out of it.

Imogene didn't tell her that she'd no schooling whatsoever. She didn't want to sink any further in the inventor's regard.

Back at the shed, Madame Lefoux gave her the tea tray. "Tell Henry to send you along with my luncheon. Enough for two, please."

Ah, thought Imogene, sadly, *the mysterious husband must be joining her.*

She returned to the house, feeling heavy, fantasizing about dimples. *Stupid dimples.*

The rest of the morning, Imogene went about her normal duties even more like a sleepwalker than before.

Henry dragged her aside mid-morning, quite cross. His hand around her arm was tight enough to bruise. "What have you done to our inventor?"

"Nothing, I swear. I only brought her the tea, as you instructed." *Although you didn't warn me not to disturb her work.* It occurred to Imogene then to resent Henry. Had he known what would happen? Was he being intentionally malicious?

The footman planted his feet and stared down his nose at her. He was tall, like all good footmen ought to be. The Woolsey Hive took care in choosing its male staff – their footmen all matched in height and hair color. "Well, Drone Lefoux just came by the kitchens, which she *never* does, to make certain you had delivered the message about her luncheon tray."

Imogene shrugged. "Surely she only wished to ensure there was enough food for herself and her husband? It has naught to do with me."

Henry's frown deepened. "Don't be ridiculous. There is no husband."

Imogene felt a wave of relief crash through her body. Not that it signified. Not that she could hope that it meant Madame Lefoux was something like her. But she did hope. Because, God, those dimples and those eyes and that lean body and the waistcoat which Imogene would unbutton slowly and the tiny bit of white throat where the top button was open which would be soft under her lips and… *STOP!*

Henry was railing. "Are you trying to steal my duties? *I* service the lab, not the parlourmaid. This morning was meant to be an exception. I was desperate because Monty is out sick, and you were here. Now she comes by special to make sure it's you again? What are you after? I knew you were a crafty bit of baggage."

Imogene was hurt by such an unwarranted accusation. "I didn't do anything!"

"So, why is she now showing you such particular

attention? It can't be interest. She's never shown *that* kind of interest in any of us, male or female."

Imogene felt heat suffuse her body. Joy. Possibility. And a reluctance to accept that it might mean anything, because what could someone so glorious see in her? She could do nothing more than hold her secret wanting close, away from Henry's prying.

"Are you after her, girl? Couldn't catch the hive's eye, so now you're going for the next level down? Sway those shapely hips about, blink those long lashes. I know the type. Here I thought you was setting your cap at me with those big dark eyes, but now…"

Imogene straightened. She knew how she was supposed to react to that; it was scripted into her head like a play she'd memorized but had yet to perform. "I'm sure I don't know *what* you mean! I'm a good girl. And I begin to suspect you're making a disgusting suggestion. I'm sorry if you thought I was leading you on. I don't know what the inventor is after. Perhaps she simply wants better company, if this is how you behave."

"Why, you opportunistic little bitch!" Henry looked as though he might lunge at her.

Imogene narrowed her eyes. "I wouldn't if I were you. We both know the vampires don't hold with bruises administered by others. They don't like pre-tenderized meat."

Henry glared at her.

Imogene tried to mediate the situation. She couldn't afford to have a first footman set against her.

Why so angry? Was he jealous? Of her or of the inventor? Had he really guessed her nature? No, not possible. Henry was not so perceptive. Then again, she'd never had to hide her attraction as well as her nature; perhaps she was not so good at that. Perhaps arrogance wouldn't be enough. *I will have to be so careful. But I will not give up the opportunity to be around her. I can't!*

Imogene said, quietly, "I'll simply explain to her that I'm not available further when I take out the luncheon tray."

That seemed to mollify Henry, although Imogene felt all the worse for a sacrifice she hadn't yet made.

"Oh, good, you're back. Put that down, would you? I could use another set of hands." The inventor was squatting behind her large engine-thing. Her eyes flashed one appreciative look up, before returning to her work. But it was unclear whether she was appreciating Imogene or the machine or the food tray.

Imogene put the tray down on top of the schematics and made her way carefully through the chaos.

"Would you pass me the driver coil, please?" Madame Lefoux was back in her leather apron and helmet. Her sleeves were rolled higher and tighter and Imogene noticed, in the flickering of the orange lighting, that her arms were quite muscled. *I thought only peasant girls had muscles.*

She cast about and spotted a tool that looked like two long curls of metal and passed that over. Madame

Lefoux took it and instantly started using it. Which Imogene supposed meant it was the requested driver coil.

After a few long moments, the inventor passed it back. "The aether sensitivity tube, please."

There was a glass vial full of some gas that, when Imogene picked it up and tilted it to the side, could possibly be grey in color.

She passed that over.

"Thank you, Miss Hale. You're good at this. Have you worked in a laboratory before?"

"No, ma'am. Uh. No, Madame. Never even seen one before today."

The inventor scooted herself out from behind her contraption and stood. A strange flicker of movement suggested she would like to reach out and touch Imogene. *I must be mistaken.*

"Well, you have a certain skill. And this is nothing. You should have seen my old contrivance chamber. A work of art." Her face stuttered into a still sadness. "It was conscripted by a herd of bossy werewolves. Such a waste." She pulled off her gloves. "Regardless, thank you for the assistance. That is stable enough for now. Did you bring food?"

"Yes, Madame, as ordered."

"Enough for two?"

"Yes, Madame." Imogene looked around for the possible guest.

"Then you shall join me."

"Oh no, Madame."

"Why not? You are hungry, no?"

"It wouldn't be proper!" Imogene was shocked.

To have been shown favor earlier that day with an arm and a short walk might be considered a mere whimsical informality from an eccentric genius. To sit down and eat a midday meal with the inventor made them equals.

Madame Lefoux walked briskly over to the desk. "Nonsense. No one need know." She leaned her bony frame over and brushed a pile of wire shavings off a stool, drawing it up to the desk. "There you go. It is no proper dining table, but it will do." It made for an intimate arrangement, crowded together by all the devices looming around them.

Lacking any other option, Imogene sat.

The food was good, and generous, slices of cold pork pie with pickled onion and green beans, followed by apple baked whole with spices. It was certainly better than Imogene's regular midday fare. Not to say the staff ate poorly – they had full roast once a week! Vampires believed in keeping their servants well fed for the sake of everyone's health, but meals rarely varied from the wholesome stew arena. Rumor was (now that Imogene knew to pay attention and keep her ears perked) that Madame Lefoux and the countess were not friendly. The inventor's indenture was a punishment and she was exiled to the countryside under sufferance. But this clearly did not extend to any kind of gastric mistreatment.

Perhaps, Imogene found herself wishing despite reality, *someday we will be friendly enough for her to tell me what happened.*

They talked easily of less private matters, the hissing hum of machinery in the background.

Madame Lefoux explained, eyes sparkling with excitement, about her latest project. Imogene looked with equally bright eyes at the schematics and calculations. There was one for an airship in the mix! Unfortunately, Madame Lefoux explained, she wasn't working on the dirigible itself, just a part for its engine. Imogene tried hard to understand, and she thought she asked the right questions, for Madame Lefoux only became more animated, her movements joyful and quick, speaking rapidly. Imogene even spotted an error on the slate of mathematics, although she hadn't the courage to point it out.

It was wonderful. And Madame Lefoux was glorious. Imogene wondered if that passion spread elsewhere in the inventor's life.

Imogene caught herself touching her hair, self-consciously. For the first time, she actually wanted to be found beautiful. And sometimes, those green eyes did linger.

Nevertheless, Imogene spent most of the time looking for an opportunity to explain that they couldn't do this again. Henry had forbidden it. She was willing to accept exile from this small corner of the hive world. Willing, because she was terrified by all the possibilities the inventor represented, and dangerously fascinated by the smudges and the dimples.

Madame Lefoux smelled of vanilla and machine oil.

Imogene couldn't believe how charming the scent was. It was also adorable the way she forgot, until fully halfway through the meal, that she still wore her helmet.

The inventor laughed at herself and took it off, putting it aside. "Excuse my poor manners, I lose myself in work."

Imogene shook her head and allowed a small smile.

The inventor's eyes lit. "There! I knew it."

Imogene lost the smile to nerves at once. "I'm sorry, Madame. I didn't…"

"No, I like it. You are such a grave young lady."

"No lady me, just a country lass."

"I think perhaps a bit more than that. You have no flock of children clutching at your skirts. You have come here instead. There is something different about you. About your choices. No?"

Imogene was terrified by this suggestion. She didn't want to be seen as anything out of the ordinary. "Ma needed the money, Madame. Not to be crass."

The inventor waved her free hand in the air while she ate pork pie. "No fear there. The British conversational custom of subject avoidance makes little sense to me."

"Pardon?"

"No need to apologize for mentioning money to a Frenchwoman."

"You speak English better than I do."

The dimples flashed. "I spent a deal of my childhood here. Well, back and forth, really. But we were talking about you."

I'd rather not.

The inventor was intent. "There are other ways

you could have helped your family. Marriage, for example – you are of the age."

"Ma calls me long in the tooth."

The inventor frowned. "You cannot be more than twenty?" And then, on a quiet note under her breath, "Far too young, really."

For some reason, this gave Imogene pride in her age, where she'd felt shame in the past. "I'm nearer thirty." Well, twenty-eight *was* nearer. "Why, how old are you?"

A quick movement of Madame Lefoux's wrist met that, up over her face, to disguise some flicker of emotion. "Thirty-seven."

Only nine years' difference, thought Imogene smugly. *Plenty of men are nine years older than their wives.* Now, that was an odd thought. *Is Madame Lefoux husband material? Ma would be so proud: at last my unmarried eldest looks to secure a gentleman's affections. Well, yes, if all gentlemen were like Madame Lefoux, wouldn't we all wish to secure them?*

Imogene suppressed the mad need to giggle and said hurriedly, "A husband and children, I always felt, weren't for me."

"Indeed? And why is that?"

Imogene blushed and didn't answer. Instead, emboldened, she asked, "Why not for you? Or is there a Mr Lefoux hiding somewhere in this mess of a lab?"

"Aha! There is pertness underneath your gravitas." The inventor seemed more delighted by Imogene's refusal to answer than offended by the impertinence. "Messy, is it? Feel the urge to clean, do you, my lovely parlourmaid? Well, you and your duster-wielding ilk are to stay out. I like my mess."

Imogene began to enjoy herself. "Evidently."

The dimples reappeared. "So, how came you to be working here, Miss Hale?"

"I believe the countess found me pretty."

"I am sure she did."

Imogene desperately wanted that gleam in the inventor's green eyes to mean that she too thought Imogene pretty. Imogene didn't care for anyone else's good opinion.

"And she likes pretty things." Imogene endeavored to explain and in so doing understand the vampire queen's greed.

"That she does. But you?"

Imogene gave a tiny smile. "I like pretty things too."

The inventor laughed, a rich, rolling sound.

It made Imogene shiver slightly. "You know what I mean, Madame. What else is there for a girl who won't marry but to go into service?"

"Will not marry or *cannot* marry?"

Imogene didn't understand the implication, so she didn't answer, taking a bite of baked apple instead. It was an odd sensation, but as she ate, she began to feel awake at last. As if it were only here, in a profoundly messy shed-laboratory, that she had any sensation of being aware and alive. That until now she'd drifted, like one of Madame Lefoux's airships. Here she felt grounded. Or at least tethered to Madame Lefoux's version of reality. *And I shall have to leave it because of Henry's envy.*

"Ah, pardon. I am being intrusive." And then on a mutter to herself, *"Ta gueule, Genevieve."*

The inventor rubbed her own forehead with one finger, adding a new smudge. And then she blurted as though she couldn't stop herself, "Would you come back again, bringing the tray? I like you better than Henry, and you were so useful earlier, with the tools and such, and..." She trailed off. For the first time, awkward. "I should like more of your help. Please."

Imogene hung her head. The last thing she wished to do was disappoint this woman. "I'm sorry, but I don't think I can get out of my other duties."

The inventor nodded, consciously controlling herself, recovering her elegance, unperturbed by rejection.

Because she is above it? Or because she doesn't care? Or because she is accustomed to it? Imogene watched those green eyes for clues. There were none.

"It's only that I used to have Quesnel for help. Now I have no one to..." Madame Lefoux drifted off. The dimples vanished.

Imogene bit her lip. Frightened of the dark turn. Had he died, this Quesnel? "You lost him?" Her voice was soft with concern.

The inventor pressed a hand to Imogene's upper arm. Imogene's skin prickled at the touch, which was *absurd*. She ruthlessly squashed the sensation.

"Oh, nothing so grave. He is away at university. My son."

Imogene blinked. "Your son!" Then there really had once been a Mr Lefoux.

The dimples returned and the inventor looked

misty-eyed. "Scamp of a boy. Well, *man*, I suppose I should call him now he's sixteen. Gone to L'École des Arts et Métiers. In Paris. Where else?" There was real pride in her voice.

Imogene had to assume that was some sort of university for brilliant inventor types. "Takes after his mother?"

"This mother, in any event."

Which statement made no sense.

Sometimes I feel I understand her perfectly, and sometimes the words are English but she might as well be speaking her native tongue. Nevertheless, Imogene nodded. She did not want to be thought a dunce.

"Look at me rambling on and on. I must get back to the counterstate conductor."

"And I must get back to work. Henry will be angry with me."

"Ah. Is that the problem?" Madame Lefoux seemed to brighten.

Imogene only stood. This was all impossible. Everything she wanted was impossible.

"Tomorrow, then, you will bring me my tea? In the morning?"

Imogene shook her head. "I cannot."

"Henry would not like it?"

Imogene said nothing, only brushed crumbs and soot off her pinafore and collected the tray.

"We must not upset Henry?" Madame Lefoux pressed.

"He is my superior," Imogene tried to explain.

"I did not imagine Henry had such a fondness for me or his duties with respect to my good self. I thought visiting the laboratory was more a hardship for him." The inventor's eyes narrowed. "We shall see what we can do about it."

Imogene was both thrilled and horrified by that statement.

CHAPTER THREE

In Which Equations Prove Fruitful and Multiply

The next morning, Henry shoved the tea tray at Imogene with a snarl. "You're to deliver her meals from here on out. I don't know how you weaseled your way in there, but you won't last any longer than your predecessor."

For good measure, he pinched Imogene's bottom, hard. Her hands were full, so she couldn't defend herself. She squeaked a protest.

Skoot, who was lurking about begging for scraps, hunched up and growled.

My stalwart protector.

Henry ignored the tiny dog. "It's not like anyone is going to know. We've all noticed how the fangs won't touch you. Not even Ambrose. And he touches everyone. I can bruise you as much as I please."

Wonderful. Imogene began to plan how to avoid being alone with the first footman. Skoot clearly wasn't enough protection. Poor silly thing. He'd taken quite a liking to Imogene, perhaps because she was the only one who gave him any affection. A pat here or there as she made her rounds, the occasional table scrap, and he was her devoted swain.

"You know, Skoot," she said as they left the kitchen. "You're one gentleman whose attentions I don't mind a'tall." With Skoot she didn't need to watch her speech. She could let the words run into each other, round and country. Not that hers was a particularly strong accent. She'd paid as close attention as she could to the gentry when they visited her village. But she'd never been taught to speak properly, just picked it up as she could.

Skoot couldn't stay with her all the time, of course. He was a very valuable and beautiful dog, for all he was quite ridiculous. The vampires might not genuinely like the Papillon, but he was theirs and must be present for them to observe of an evening.

However it was daylight, so when Imogene took out Madame Lefoux's tea, Skoot acted as her small, feathery, brown-and-white escort. Her bum smarted and her pride was nearly as sore. But Imogene was happier knowing she would see the inventor regularly.

It was all for naught. Madame Lefoux wasn't there. The shed was locked. More to the point, it was *silent*.

One of the gardeners saw her and Skoot wandering about with the tray.

"Won't do you any good, lass. Sometimes she's like that. Gets all caught up late into the night, then sleeps the morning away. Take it back – she'll ring if she wants it later."

So, Imogene took it back. (Skoot stayed with the gardeners. One of them offered him a mutton bone to gnaw on. Skoot was easily distracted by mutton.) Henry was still there and pinched her again. In the same place.

Imogene wanted to shove her feather duster up his nose. And twirl.

She did see the inventor at luncheon. Imogene's cheeks flushed in excitement, but Madame Lefoux was quite distracted and paid her little mind beyond common courtesy. When Imogene put down the tray, the inventor did look up and smile. Imogene gave her a wide grin back.

This seemed to cause Madame Lefoux some kind of pain, or perhaps it was the contraption she worked on, because she flinched and swore softly, adding under her breath, *"Je suis dans le pétrin."*

Imogene quickly hid her own enthusiasm, embarrassed. She arranged everything as best she could. Lingering, hoping to be asked to help. But the full force of that intellect wasn't turned on her, and she was not invited to stay.

Imogene was disappointed but not surprised. She'd known yesterday's informality must be an aberration. That joy of attention and inquiry could not possibly be repeated between two women of such differing classes and education. This was good enough, Imogene reassured herself. *I shall see her every day.* Many did not get even that much.

"Thank you, dear," Madame Lefoux said without looking up. "I am set for the rest of the afternoon. You may return to your duties."

"Of course, Madame." Imogene was grateful for the other woman's absentmindedness; her own brain felt swollen and foolish.

"Miss Hale?"

"Yes, Madame?"

"When you come back for the empty tray, just let yourself in and take it away. I have a delicate experiment to conduct. I would rather not be disturbed."

"Certainly, Madame."

Imogene returned a few hours later, duties permitting, pleased to find Madame Lefoux had not been so distracted that she forgot to eat. Imogene suspected, given the inventor's lean frame, that kind of thing happened all too often.

She paused to watch the woman work. The inventor was so graceful, performing some intricate and exotic dance with her machinery and tools. No sparks this time, simply the rhythmic clunk of an engine in motion, accompanied by occasional bursts of white steam. A twist here, an adjustment there, fast and sure, and then a long pause to shovel coal, every movement practiced and elegant.

Wait. She's feeding the boilers herself? Surely the hive can afford to hire her a sootie. To relieve some of the hard labor. Then again, perhaps Madame Lefoux enjoyed back-breaking work. She certainly had the muscles for it. Or perhaps a precise amount of coal was required to maintain a specific temperature and she dared not trust anyone else.

Imogene watched for as long as she felt was polite. Her gaze was drawn to the nape of the inventor's neck. It was exposed when she bent her head. Imogene itched to touch. Something was on her skin just there – between her aggressively short hair and the top of her collar, mostly hidden behind the fabric.

A birthmark, perhaps? A bite? Imogene felt her heart sink all the way to her stomach. *Please, not a bite mark.*

She didn't know why the idea was so horrible. *We are all of us here, even Madame Lefoux, in the hive's thrall. Why should she be exempt come snack time?* But until that moment, Imogene had thought of the inventor as somehow apart from all that. Unsullied. Or even, just possibly, cursed by the same affliction as she. She'd hoped that they shared something which made them both unwanted by vampires for bed or breakfast.

Imogene turned away (avoiding the possibility of a bite), her eye falling on the large slate hanging next to the desk.

Her brain did what it always did when fretful. It sank into the safety of the numbers scribbled there. She didn't entirely understand the details of those complex... *What did Madame Lefoux call them? Equations?* But some of the sums were simple enough. Division, multiplication, addition, and subtraction – those she knew, those she understood.

It had been niggling at her – one column to the far right side, near the bottom of the slate.

It must be a mistake. There was no way (not that she knew of) that the world allowed that particular string of numbers to result in the final solution written beneath. A factor of ten had been miscarried.

She glanced over, wondering if she should say something. But the inventor had said explicitly that she did not wish to be disturbed.

So, because she couldn't help herself – *The numbers are wrong!* – Imogene picked up a small stick of chalk, wiped out the error with her sleeve, and made the fix. *There.*

It looked right. The world was in order once more. Her nerves were calmed.

Then, guilty, she placed the chalk exactly where it had been and, whisking up the empty tray, scuttled from the shed. She closed the door carefully behind her.

Little did she know the consequences of that tiny adjustment with a piece of chalk. In fact, she'd quite forgotten about it by the time it returned to haunt her.

Madame Lefoux remained focused and occupied the rest of that week. She was gracious to Imogene when she entered, but she was also stiff, even a little cool.

Imogene berated herself. *I smiled too big. I showed too much. She senses my warped nature. The things I hide. She's disgusted by me. But she made a fuss insisting that I serve her and now she can't get out of it.*

Imogene tried not to pine overmuch. Well, she

pined a little. She couldn't help it; Madame Lefoux was so exactly perfect. And sometimes, although this was surely wishful thinking, she thought she caught a look, a quick glance, of such hunger. It was as though the inventor were starving and Imogene the meal, only a meal Madame Lefoux could barely allow herself to look at, let alone taste.

So, Imogene kept her smiles to herself, kept her hands from trembling, and tried to quiet the excited beating of her heart, as if Madame Lefoux were some werewolf to hear the catches in her breath. Instead, she was all efficiency, making sure the inventor ate, as much as she could without being intrusive. She wanted very badly to take care of her. She adored the times when she was summoned to help, to pass over tools, or to assist with lifting some heavy piece of machinery. She would gladly have done more. Her work as parlourmaid was lighter and certainly cleaner than anything in the potting shed. But the laboratory was so interesting. She began to see some of the patterns that drove the inventor. To understand, in a limited way, why something might fit together and work and something else might not.

On Sunday, Imogene had the day off to visit her family. She'd little interest in the obligation, but someone needed to deliver her earnings, and she'd nothing else to do.

She found her mother abed and the littles running ragged through the village, but everyone was looking better then they had in a long while. There'd even been a little meat that week.

"Due to your contribution, dear," Ma explained.

Imogene bustled about the house, cleaning as she could, preparing a meal. Ma was disposed to nervous spells, had been ever since Imogene was old enough to do most of the heavy lifting.

"Is it horrible there, dear?" Ma asked as if she half hoped it were.

"No, it's passable."

Ma didn't look convinced. "May I see?" She made a finger motion to her own neck.

Imogene went over, bent down, and pulled aside the ruffle about her throat. It was her Sunday best. Not that she could attend church anymore now that she worked for vampires, but it was her best. A pretty chintz, perhaps a tad frayed and tight, but she thought she looked well in it. And maybe she'd walked away from the big house past Madame Lefoux's shed… just in case.

"No bites. You *are* a lucky girl."

"They don't seem to want me." Imogene didn't try to explain.

"Thank the stars," breathed her mother. She recovered some color in her cheeks.

"Now," said Imogene, "can you manage a little broth?" Considering Ma's affliction was more likely imagined than reality, Imogene hoped it might be cured by the application of sustenance. People always seemed emotionally fortified when they sipped warm liquids.

They'd settled into a pattern on Sundays. Imogene did what she could around the house.

Showed her mother proof that no vampires were feeding on her, told the littles a story, then wended her way back.

She'd yet to mention Madame Lefoux. Imogene didn't want to share her, not even by proxy. More important, she wasn't certain she could hide her interest. What was there to tell, anyway? Nothing of consequence. The inventor had shown no true favor beyond requesting her service, had given Imogene no more marked attention. She was a naturally amiable woman. Any casual affection must be considered the result of her being French. Imogene tried to keep herself from wanting more than that.

But she found herself wanting quite a bit more. No doubt Ma would sense this wistfulness if she spoke of the inventor at all. Mothers were tricky like that. Best to keep Madame Lefoux a secret alongside everything else.

When Imogene returned to the big house that evening, there was a spring in her step. Her family was as well as she could make them, and tomorrow she would get to see Madame Lefoux again.

Unfortunately, the hive was in an uproar.

Imogene hurried to change into her pinafore and assume Greta's duties. The evening parlourmaid was off to visit a sick aunt, or ailing uncle, or malnourished goldfish, or some such excuse. In fact, she was walking out with one of the under-gardeners. No one was supposed to know, but the entirety of belowstairs was very well aware. Imagine, *outside*

help pairing with *inside* staff? Shocking.

Imogene shuddered to think what they would say if they ever knew her fantasies. An upstairs maid with one of the quality? Both of them girls! She tortured herself with the idea of cool hands and engineered calluses.

When she emerged from the servants' wing, it was to find the household in chaos.

Madame Lefoux was striding about, ranting at the top of her lungs. "I want him found! *Tout de suite!* Whoever it was, I want him located this instant!" She was in a fury about something. Imogene had never seen her like this. Her green eyes fairly flashed, and her accent had gone quite strong.

"Bring me all the musicians currently in residence. It is *always* musicians. Cannot keep themselves to themselves and tend to be better at mathematics than anyone else. Well! Well! Where are they?"

What was she on about? Imogene was splendid at sums and couldn't carry a tune to save her life. She inched closer, duster twirling innocently.

The butler attempted to calm the inventor. "Please, Madame Lefoux, try to contain yourself. The sun is nearly set. We cannot possibly have the vampires awakening to this sort of carrying on. If you would consider the conservatory?"

"The conservatory? The conservatory! Why should I consider that?"

"If you would adjourn there? I will have the footmen round up all the musicians currently in residence and send them to you."

"This minute?"

"Yes, Madame. Right this very minute. Except Mr Wetherston-Ponsford. He is performing this evening."

"Is he indeed? Do you happen to know if Mr Wetherston-Ponsford has a penchant for arithmetic?"

The butler took serious offense to such an accusation being leveled at the absent (and thus unable to mount a defense) Mr Wetherston-Ponsfords of the world. "Now, Madame, do you think you should go around casting aspersions on perfectly decent pianists like that?"

Madame Lefoux gave the man a disgusted, very French-seeming wave of the hand and then stomped off, presumably to the conservatory. Imogene thought that a stomping Madame Lefoux was the most fiercely adorable thing she'd ever seen.

The butler looked harried.

Imogene presented herself for inspection. "Sir?"

"Where's Greta?"

"She's off this evening, sir. Visiting someone sick, I believe."

"Oh, yes, of course. Well, come along, then. There's dusting to do."

"Sir, what's wrong with Madame Lefoux?"

"Someone tinkered with one of her precious equations. She is on a rampage trying to discover whom. Hence the musicians. Apparently, they're supposed to be good with numbers. Although, if you ask me, a lady ought to be careful hurling accusations of mathematics around all willy-nilly like that. I blame the French."

Imogene felt as if she might faint. *But I fixed it days ago. She only now noticed?* She wondered if she should go confess straight away, collect her dismissal, and have done with it. Clearly, she'd botched up everything.

But she was a coward.

Nevertheless, Imogene found that her parlourmaid's duties that night took her more and more frequently into the vicinity of the conservatory, where Madame Lefoux was running an inquisition in a startlingly Spanish manner for a Frenchwoman.

Imogene wouldn't have thought a mere indenture outranked the household's true drones. But Madame Lefoux certainly acted as though she had ultimate authority. The drones seemed frightened enough by her wrath to do as requested. There were two pianists, one harpist, one violinist, and a tuba player residing at the hive currently. (Imogene had heard the tuba player practicing and thought it sounded remarkably like flatulence, but apparently, this was highly regarded in some circles.) With one of the pianists already gone, Madame Lefoux could only terrorize the remaining four musicians. She put them to a round of questioning and then set them some sums.

Everyone ended up frustrated by the impromptu examinations.

"Are you positive it was not any of you?" The inventor stood, hands on hips.

She'd changed for supper. Imogene had never before seen her out of work clothes. She looked very well, scrubbed clean and wearing a suit of moss green, with an emerald waistcoat, and a silver cravat. The hands on hips pinched in her clothing, emphasizing her tiny waist. She was so lean, Imogene sometimes wondered if there were curves there at all. What she wouldn't give to find out.

The musician drones were nowhere near as terrified as Imogene would have been in their place, seeming instead mostly annoyed.

In the end, Madame Lefoux had to let them go.

"Flighty as opera dancers," was her rude remark to their departing backs.

Imogene found her way to dusting the potted plants in one corner of the room.

Madame Lefoux tilted her head back and stared at the glass ceiling in exasperation.

"Perhaps," she said, apparently to herself, "it was one of the keepers? But why come into my laboratory and do nothing more than change a sum? Do I have a technology spy on my hands? Professor Swern is pursuing the same line of inquiry. He would give a gold-dusted diamond-roodle to see my notes. But even so, why reveal himself by tinkering with an equation?"

Imogene piped up. "Did it mess everything up horribly, then?"

Madame Lefoux whirled. Seeing who it was, she smiled. Her whole demeanor altered, those impossibly green eyes narrowed, focusing entirely on Imogene. "A very good evening to you, Miss Hale. I did not see you for tea today. Or luncheon, for that matter."

"It's my day off, Madame."

"Then why are you here… dusting?"

"The other parlourmaid has the evening off."

"Indeed? Do you ever actually get an entire day of liberty?"

Imogene frowned. What an odd notion. "No, Madame. Of course not. I'm in service."

The inventor shook her head, looking sad. "Naturally. How silly of me. Now, what did you ask?"

"I asked if it was very wrong, what was done to your equation."

Madame Lefoux pursed her lips. "No, no, in fact, quite the opposite. It was very right. I completed the prototype as a result. I had a factor off and it was throwing everything into chaos. At some point, someone fixed it, and I proceeded without realizing. This resulted in a working counterstate aetheric conductor at last. Well, theoretically working, I'll need to take it floating to test it properly."

"Then why do you wish to punish the, uh, equation bandit?"

"Punish? *Punish!* What a preposterous idea. I thought to recruit. Once in a while, you understand, I require help with calculations. Mathematics are not my strongest suit." Madame Lefoux was beginning to regard Imogene with a crafty expression.

Imogene knew she was blushing hotly.

She screwed her courage to the sticking point. It wasn't that she thought she might actually be any good. She didn't, after all, understand the equations themselves, couldn't even read them. But the inventor deserved to know the truth.

"It was me."

Madame Lefoux grinned in delight. Slaying

Imogene with those deadly dimples. "I was hoping you were working yourself up to that. And now I recall your asking about the equation that first day we met. Did you spot the error, even then?"

Imogene nodded.

"And, poor thing, you had to work up the courage to fix it? And believed you had to hide it from me? Am I so fierce a creature?"

"Oh no! It's only, I didn't want to be thought interfering."

"Interfering, indeed. *Belle amie*, you've saved me weeks of work! I only wish you had done it the moment you noticed it."

Imogene could not have been more honored. She knew her cheeks must be crimson with pleasure. "I shall not hesitate again."

"What is it you English say? That is the spirit!" Madame Lefoux strode over and patted her on the back, despite the duster that Imogene now twirled nervously between two hands.

The inventor seemed to remember herself and quickly stopped touching Imogene. "Perhaps I was a tad severe on the musicians."

Imogene didn't say anything, but her expression must have spoken volumes.

"Bah. Do them good. Now, how is it you knew my answer was wrong?"

Imogene gave a self-deprecating shrug. "I like sums. I've always been good with them."

"What is three hundred and eighty-six plus forty-seven?"

"Four hundred and thirty-three," answered

Imogene promptly.

"Remarkable," the inventor practically crowed. She cast about for another one. Then gave Imogene some subtraction. Then multiplication. Then division. Imogene answered everything correctly, although Madame Lefoux didn't bother to check, simply assumed she was right.

"I knew a boy at university like you. It is a gift, you know?"

Imogene paled a little. "Is it artistic?"

Madame Lefoux frowned. "Excellent question. I do not know. Best not to tell the vampires. Unless you are interested in immortality?"

Imogene shook her head violently. She'd no desire to live longer than one lifetime; her current one was confusing enough.

"I quite agree." The inventor was empathetic. Which explained, in part, why she was an indenture and not a real drone.

"I can simply claim that, with Quesnel gone, I need a little extra help in my laboratory and that you and I get along well. That should keep the queen from concerning herself."

"But I'm only a parlourmaid."

The inventor waved a hand. "Bah. Someone else can dust."

That's not the point. I'm not worthy of helping. But Imogene didn't say that. How to explain the English class system to a willfully obtuse Frenchwoman? Madame Lefoux had already shown little regard for the sanctity of musicians.

Imogene had to admit that it was thrilling, the

idea that she might be of assistance to an inventor's genius. And terrifying that they would share intimate quarters in the shed for longer than they already were.

Madame Lefoux frowned. "It will have to be Dr Caedes I petition. I know he is vile, but he is the easiest to manipulate. He thinks we share an interest. He fancies himself an engineer." Her tone of voice suggested she found the vampire wanting in that regard.

Imogene nodded mutely. She didn't know Dr Caedes personally, had only met him a few times. He, like the other vampires, was not awake during her working day.

He had a reputation amongst the maids for coming up to the servants' quarters to *check* and make certain there was no unlicensed fraternization. His *checking* usually involved interrupting the maids during their bathing hour. Imogene had been very quick about her bath since hearing that.

"Come along, then, no time like the present." Madame Lefoux went to guide her forward with a hand to her back. Imogene tensed in delighted anticipation. Then the inventor shook herself and simply gestured with that hand for Imogene to precede her from the room.

Imogene stood before Dr Caedes in his private sitting room and tried not to tremble. The burr in the man's voice was spiked with annoyance.

"I'm only just up, you vile female. What on earth could you possibly want?" His thin frame and considerable height were emphasized by a long house robe. It was deep red silk, very expensive. It draped in such a way as to emphasize the fact that he wore nothing underneath.

Imogene found this grotesque and suspiciously intentional. Did he wish to put visitors on edge? Or was he simply the kind of man who liked to expose himself?

Madame Lefoux was not impressed. "I want her," she said, pointing at Imogene.

Imogene was standing, hands clasped before her, head slightly bent, trying not look at the red robe. This bald statement was too much. She was forced to raise her eyes. Surely, the vampire would be shocked by such a statement.

But the doctor only sneered, unsurprised. "Well, you can have her and be done with it. What's that to me?"

Madame Lefoux looked mortified. "Oh, dear me, no. I was not…" She turned to Imogene. "No offense meant, Miss Hale. I am not… I would never take advantage like that! That is, she is not…" The inventor took a moment to collect herself. "I want her to assist me with my work."

Imogene knew she was nearly as red as that appalling robe. Now she was being rejected as undesirable in front of a vampire.

Said vampire gave an exaggerated sigh. "Why on earth would you want this country bumpkin in your laboratory? For goodness' sake, woman, find yourself some nice young university chap." He licked his lips. "Perhaps one of the rosy blonds they produce in the south. Strapping. Big... teeth. Proper blue blood and a good education is what you need." His lip curled. "And male. You can't waste your time on *that*." He waved a hand at Imogene. Who was looking at her feet. "I wager she can't even read. Can you, girl?"

Silence.

"Well?"

Imogene's voice was barely above a whisper. "No, sir." Couldn't he just eat her and be done with it? It'd be less painful.

"There, see?" The vampire's tone was smug.

Madame Lefoux's eyes narrowed.

Imogene was beginning to realize that her inventor was not the kind of woman who tolerated having her will thwarted.

"I do not want anyone with his own agenda or outside interests. This girl will suit me perfectly. I merely require an extra pair of hands."

"Then I shall assign you one of the footmen."

"No, they are bumbling fools."

"Not *our* footmen, or I shall know the reason why."

Madame Lefoux looked close to losing her temper again. "I want *this girl*. Why are you being difficult about it?"

"Why do you want her in particular?"

"She is quiet and calm and she does not interfere."

The vampire looked back and forth between the two. "You want to seduce her?"

Madame Lefoux let out a breath. "Just because your mind is in the gutter, Doctor, does not mean mine so resides."

The vampire stood at that. Looming. He let his fangs show in annoyance. Madame Lefoux was not his equal, she was only an indenture, and she'd taken things too far.

"Request denied!" he said. "Now get out!"

CHAPTER FOUR

In Which Werewolves Come Calling

Madame Lefoux puffed out her cheeks. "Well, that did not go well. I do not understand why he was so insistent. It is possible he has his eye on you, *choupinette*. I should be careful if I were you. Lock your door at night."

"Servants aren't allowed padlocks."

"No? Of course they aren't." The inventor gritted her teeth. "Then wedge some furniture against the knob."

"Yes, Madame."

"Miss Hale, I am sorry that did not work out."

"Me as well. I should have liked to be of assistance. I still will try, when I bring you your tray. If you've something you need me to calculate."

"We need more time than that. I want to teach you the whole theory of algebraic mathematics. Then I can throw the entire slate at you, and you can find my mistakes."

That sounded glorious to Imogene. The moment she'd first seen that slate, she'd wished for nothing more than to understand it. Well, maybe a few things more.

"We will have to formulate another strategy. I have not given up yet!"

Imogene smiled. Then tried not to notice that this made Madame Lefoux flinch. "I appreciate your faith in me. He was right, you know. I can't read."

Madame Lefoux waved that off. "Then I shall teach you. You are a smart girl. You would apply yourself."

"Diligently. I'd be the first in my family. It'd be an honor."

Madame Lefoux looked sad. "For now, we must bide our time. I may have miscalculated, bringing you to the hive's attention."

"I'm not afraid of them," said Imogene, staunchly.

"No, you aren't. Why is that?"

Because they could never be worse than the thing I fear I already am. Imogene shrugged.

"Very well, keep your own counsel." The inventor ran a hand through her short, wavy hair distractedly. "About that other thing. It was badly done. You know I am not" – she winced – "like him in that way?"

"Pardon?" Imogene didn't follow.

"A predator."

Of course not. You're no vampire. "I never thought you were."

Madame Lefoux stumbled on, strangely unsure

of herself. "You are too young, even if it were not a breach of trust. And, of course, you have shown no inclination."

"I'm twenty-nine, as of yesterday," objected Imogene. She knew she didn't look her age, but in this she wished to be clear. It seemed to matter a great deal to the inventor.

"Oh, dear me. Your birthday? I did not know."

Imogene tilted her head. "It's of no consequence. Another year has passed."

"Still, that does complicate matters."

Imogene blinked. "It does?" She'd thought her being older than she looked would be a good thing. But now Madame Lefoux seemed even more worried. She was nibbling her lower lip with fine white teeth.

"You are a parlourmaid."

I know!

"And you are an innocent."

Not for lack of trying. I joined the hive house for a reason.

"I am not inclined towards corruption."

Corrupt me, Imogene wanted to cry out. *For goodness' sake! Please?*

"And now there is Dr Caedes to consider. Oh dear, how do I get myself into these messes?" Madame Lefoux moved closer to Imogene in the hallway. It being a public thoroughfare, it was a miracle no one had yet stumbled upon their conversation.

For one glorious moment, Imogene thought (Imogene hoped) that the inventor intended to kiss her. She stopped breathing.

But it must have been a trick of the light, for instead, the inventor said, "Remember the chair under the doorknob this evening, Miss Hale."

"Yes, Madame."

Imogene remembered. For three nights running she remembered. Her roommate gave her funny looks when Imogene had to wake to let her in.

Alone, Imogene lay listening for vampire-soft footsteps. But if the doctor had his eye on her, it was from a distance.

She replayed the conversation in her head. *Madame Lefoux doesn't want to corrupt me. Does that mean she is inclined? Perhaps she wants me as I do her and it's only her scruples that keep us apart. Is it our age difference, or my position and lack of education that repulse her? Something else? Something about me?* Imogene couldn't deny that the inventor avoided touching her. But did she do that because she was disgusted, or tempted?

Imogene decided it would be better to know than not, because if the inventor was tempted, Imogene intended to be as tempting as possible.

"It's all over the house that Lefoux went after you for personal maid and was denied." Henry was positively smirking. "The fangs didn't consider you good enough for her."

Imogene concentrated on loading one of the trays. Mr Wetherston-Ponsford had ordered a repast in his private chambers.

"I didn't take you for the type to cast yourself at a tom. Yet here you are, pretty as all get-out, nose in the air. I'm thinking it's not that you believe you're too good for us lads – too good for me – it's that you ain't that particular. Did you expect to get the countess and settle for the inventor? Poor Imogene, you ain't good enough for her, either."

The scullery maid stepped out to check the washroom, leaving them alone together.

Imogene tensed.

Henry came around the table to press close – rubbing himself flush against her hip. "What you need is a lesson in sausage-making. Then you'll stop pining after a two-bit hack with nothing more upstairs than she has down below."

Imogene jabbed him with her elbow.

He hissed and backed away, but more because the scullery maid had returned than out of fear.

Imogene was fiercely angry. Not for being exposed before him (that made her scared, not angry, and he couldn't prove anything) but for his insult to Madame Lefoux's intelligence. "She is brilliant, and you're a ratbag. Are you after me because you can't catch another girl's fancy?"

The scullery maid gasped at that.

Henry was generally well regarded by the maids. He was, after all, a first footman, and vampires always traded on looks. He had a square jaw and dark hair, broad shoulders and muscled thighs. Many a lass about the kitchen would be honored to walk out with him.

Two spots of color appeared on his cheeks. Imogene wondered if she hadn't shot near the mark. Some men, and she knew it well from her village, preferred an unwilling lass.

Lovely, she thought, hoisting the tray. *Now I've two reasons to block my door at night.*

Giving them a nervous glance, the scullery maid nipped out once more.

Henry took that as an opportunity to shove Imogene towards the massive iron range. She avoided a severe burn by twisting aside, but bashed her ankle on the coal scuttle. She managed, by some miracle, not to drop the tray.

She made good her escape, but her ankle had swelled to twice its normal size by the end of the day.

She vowed to keep her mouth shut around Henry. *When I do decide to talk, it inevitably gets me into trouble.*

The next day Imogene got a glorious little stint in the potting shed at luncheon. Madame Lefoux was undertaking a new set of calculations, and she asked Imogene to look over some of the more complex sums. Everything seemed sound this time.

The inventor avoided looking at Imogene, with a will. She stiffened whenever Imogene approached, holding herself aloof.

Trying to protect me? Imogene wondered. *Or has she changed her mind? Does she regret having asked Dr Caedes for my services?* It was all so confusing.

Imogene tried to be tempting, except she'd no

experience with flirting. The boys of the village had always chased her. Even if she'd known what to do with a man, how did one tempt another woman? She tried batting her eyelashes, but the inventor never looked at her long enough to notice. Or perhaps she thought Imogene had soot in her eye.

It was over too soon. Madame Lefoux returned to absentminded mode, but she did bestow upon Imogene a dimpled smile and sincere thanks for her help. Imogene glowed with it.

The inventor touched her hair and then made a funny little sound in her throat. "Off with you now."

Imogene headed for the door.

A sudden clatter and a flutter of movement had Madame Lefoux standing next to her, one arm about her waist.

"You're hurt!" Those two words were more heavily accented than Imogene had ever heard.

Imogene's breath hitched. "I hit the coal scuttle with my ankle."

"It is not like you to be clumsy. You move like silk."

I do? She watches me move? Oh, God, she watches me move. Self-consciousness swamped her, making her shake. *What should I do?*

The inventor knelt at Imogene's feet, cool hands gently stroking her swollen ankle above the top of her old worn shoe, testing the bone. "And here I was, trying not to think about your..."

What? Imogene wanted to scream. *Trying not to think about my what?*

"I almost missed this. It doesn't seem broken.

You should stay off it and cool it in the lake."

Mute with shock, Imogene nodded. Of course, she could do neither; there was dusting to do.

The inventor's fingers lingered on her stocking-covered leg. Imogene wished the stocking to perdition. What she wouldn't give for skin on skin. She was flushed with the touch, and horrified that the inventor was kneeling at her feet!

"Madame, you shouldn't… that is… it's not right for you to…"

The other woman stood and practically leapt away. Which was absolutely not the reaction Imogene had intended. *Why do I ever open my mouth?*

"*Bordel de merde*. I am so sorry. I should never have touched you so. I do apologize."

"No," cried Imogene. "No, it's fine! I don't mind that at all, but you were kneeling at my…"

She trailed off. The inventor was backing away and muttering to herself, apparently in anger.

I should go now, decided Imogene. And so she went, feeling both crushed and elated at the same time.

When she returned to the house, Henry pinched her again. Imogene was so out of temper that she decided to miscount the silver on purpose. Let Henry explain *that* to his superiors. Unfortunately, what on most days would have been a minor annoyance threw the entire household into a tizzy, thinking someone was after werewolves.

"Don't know why they're making such a fuss. It's

only a teaspoon. Can't kill a werewolf with a teaspoon, not even a silver one," complained Henry.

"Oh, yes, young man." The butler was having none of Henry's lip, today of all days. "And what do you know about killing werewolves?"

Henry modified his tone. "Nothing, sir. Nothing at all."

Apparently the London Alpha and his lady wife were calling that very evening. Missing silver was of serious concern in any household, but especially a supernatural one. Imogene cursed herself for bad timing.

Cook found the missing spoon later (where Imogene had stashed it in the breadbox). So, trouble didn't come down on Imogene's head. At least, not in the form of a silver teaspoon.

Oh, no, it came from a different source entirely.

Imogene's shift had ended but they kept her on that evening despite her limp. All available hands were set to work; apparently these guests required a serious show of respect in quantity if not quality.

"It happens sometimes, dear." The housekeeper patted Imogene's head absently in an irritating manner.

Mrs Gladstone was a strict taskmistress but fair and kind at elusive moments – a mannish female, with a set mouth and crooked teeth. One wouldn't have thought her the vampires' type, except that she moved with such grace – her neck long and elegant, her hair pulled severely back to show cheekbones that could etch an aetherogram, and clear skin for all her advanced age. *I suppose vampires are old enough to appreciate all kinds of beauty.*

"I don't mind, ma'am," replied Imogene.

"You're a good girl. It shouldn't go too late. It's the werewolves, you see? The hive likes to put best necks forward. And Lord Maccon has an eye for a pretty, dark-haired lass. So, the queen wants all the nicest specimens on display. Including you, she specifically said." Mrs Gladstone was a true servant, not a drone, hired for her skill at household management with no expectations of trying for immortality. Nevertheless, she wholly embraced the whims of the supernatural set without question.

Madame Lefoux is pretty and dark-haired, Imogene thought. *Will she be commanded to perform this evening too? Show off some invention or another?*

It looked to be that way. Because while Imogene waited with Greta to act as receiving staff, she witnessed Madame Lefoux return from her laboratory.

Lord Ambrose accosted her in the hallway. "You're late!"

"Plenty of time, Ambrose."

"They'll be here within the hour. You're to give them proper regard. Full evening dress. Appear as you do now and they'll think we torture you. You're filthy, and your shirt sleeves are *rolled!* Are you mad, woman? Rolled shirt sleeves is taking artistic expression to an utterly unacceptable level. Not to mention the fact that you've lost weight again."

The inventor looked cross. "I've been working."

"Yes, yes. And you miss your son. Excuses, excuses. But there is no excuse for rolled sleeves! You think the muhjah will care for that? It'll be all our fault. She likes you, for all she punished you with us."

Madame Lefoux grinned. "Sometimes, I think she punished you with me."

The vampire actually smiled, showing fang. "You and me both, woman. Quickly, now!"

"Well," said Madame Lefoux to Lord Ambrose as they made their way upstairs. "I can reliably assure you that Alexia would never notice my sleeves."

Lord Ambrose gave a dry, humorless smile, by which point they were out of eavesdropping range.

Imogene was fascinated. She was also deeply suspicious of the so-called muhjah. This *Alexia* person. What right had she to *like* Madame Lefoux? Or to not notice her sleeves?

"Stop listening at doorways, Imogene," Greta hissed. "Help me with this tablecloth."

Imogene went to assist. It hardly mattered, since Madame Lefoux was now upstairs in her room.

Imogene wondered where that was. Was it near the queen's private quarters? Did she have her own chamber or did she share with another indenture? For some reason, it had never occurred to Imogene to wonder before now. She had, until this moment, conceived of Madame Lefoux as beginning and ending with the potting shed. In Imogene's mind, the inventor sprang into existence just before Imogene entered the potting shed, and then out of existence when she left it.

But no. Madame Lefoux had a room somewhere

up there.

With a bed in which she slept.

Imogene straightened the tablecloth with a yank and stopped herself forcibly from thinking in that direction. Except that she couldn't stop.

For Madame Lefoux was there now, undressing and then redressing for supper.

Who would help her with that? Who was her lady's maid? Did a woman who dressed as a man have a lady's maid or did she have a valet? Imogene found the idea of a valet less troubling. That a man might be assisting the inventor into her waistcoat and cravat was fine, but a woman…

Why is that? Imogene shook her head, frustrated with herself. *Because I want to do it* was the obvious answer. *As if I ranked lady's maid… or valet, for that matter.*

In no time at all, the guests arrived.

Given the general tizzy, Imogene might have expected the entire London Pack for supper. However, it was only the Alpha, his wife, and their Gamma.

The Gamma, as it turned out, was a familiar face. He was a big man, pale blond with icy blue eyes and the up-tilted arrogance of hidden secrets. He didn't notice her. He wasn't the type to notice staff.

Imogene kept her eyes down as she took coats and hats. Practicing the servant's art of invisibility. Greta passed around a blood-and-claret aperitif for the werewolves and vampires. Lady Maccon took tea. Imogene watched the Alpha's wife with increasing curiosity and no small measure of envy.

Countess Nadasdy did not join them. She would wait for a more formal arrangement. Lord Ambrose, being her praetoriani, stayed at her side. Thus the other two Woolsey vampires, Dr Caedes and the Duke of Hematol, entertained the guests, along with a few of the more long-standing drones. And Skoot.

The conversation was painfully polite, although the Alpha werewolf seemed to want none of it. He was grumpy and restless. His wife kept giving him exasperated looks.

Skoot was not impressed by the werewolves, or had no sense of self-preservation. During one very fraught moment, the tiny dog actually looked as if he would cock a leg over the Gamma's boots.

The werewolf in question drew back his lips and actually growled at the dog. "I have eaten your kind for less." At which Skoot finally registered the danger and went to cower in a corner. Imogene was too much on duty to offer him comfort.

"He's not lying," admitted Lady Maccon in a resigned tone, and then, "I didn't know vampires liked dogs."

Dr Caedes shrugged. "It's the country. All country houses keep dogs. And that one was the prettiest."

Such pleasantries disposed of, Lady Maccon asked, "Where is Madame Lefoux?"

Imogene tried not to look interested in the woman's evident eagerness for the company of one skinny inventor.

The dog-eating Gamma, whose name, as it turned out, was Major Channing, rolled his eyes. Apparently,

Madame Lefoux's welcome to this party was somewhat fraught.

Dr Caedes summoned Imogene with a glance, since the butler had momentarily stepped away. "Go get the inventor."

Imogene dropped a curtsy and trotted out, terrified and thrilled. Was his singling her out for this task some level of permission? Was he relaxing his stance on her helping with sums? And would she now get to see Madame Lefoux's bedroom?

The butler was directly outside in the hallway, arranging some small nibbles to be brought in with more tea.

"Sir? They want Madame Lefoux. Should I get her or would you rather?"

"I've no time for that, and the footmen are occupied with the table arrangements. You go."

"Which room, sir?"

"Madame Lefoux occupies the Crane and Chrysanthemum Room. Turn right at the top of the grand staircase, third door down on the left. Quickly, girl!"

Imogene limped off up the big stairs.

She knocked loudly and briskly, as she'd been instructed for the shed. It seemed a great deal more echoing and aggressive inside Woolsey Castle.

From behind the heavy door an aggrieved voice called for her to enter. *Perhaps a mistake. Did I knock too loud?*

Imogene wasn't sure what to expect inside, but she liked it.

The inventor's room was tidy (especially when

compared to her laboratory) and decorated in a style wholly different from every other part of the house.

Woolsey Castle boasted eight flying buttresses – an architecturally immodest choice. Imogene had grown up with Woolsey as the foremost residence in the area, but had never once heard anyone refer to it as *pretty*. Even she, who cherished no little loyalty to the castle, was realistic about its appearance. In truth, Woolsey was no castle but instead a manor house made to look like a castle, with stone facings, an excessive number of haphazardly applied turrets, crenellated battlements, extensive dungeons, and the aforementioned immodest buttresses.

Being for most of its recent history the residence of a wolf pack, the interior had fared no better. Imogene had heard reports of a true bachelor existence – if said bachelors turned to raving, slavering beasts once a month. The vampires had taken possession only to find claw-marked hardwood, gnawed banisters, no carpets at all, and the occasional bleached spot on the floorboards – which no one wanted to investigate further.

The hive had done its damnedest over the intervening years. Being the world's premier civilizing force (in a bite-your-neck-and-suck-your-blood kind of way), they insisted on plush rugs, beautiful paintings, and stunning statuary. They'd buffed, painted, and shined away all evidence of werewolf occupation. The walls were paneled in dark wood or rich jewel-toned wallpaper. The furniture was solid and mostly mahogany. The cushions and curtains were heavy velvet, and everything else brocade.

Imogene found it all lush, mildly oppressive, and highly uncomfortable. Not that she got to sit very much, but it certainly looked uncomfortable.

Madame Lefoux's room was *entirely* different.

The walls had been papered in a pale green with bright birds and flowers of some exotic overseas style. The furniture was a light wood – *easy to clean, how nice of her*. The curtains were white and filmy, allowing for the extensive view of the grounds to be displayed to maximum advantage and giving the chamber the general feeling of cheerful airiness. Imogene imagined it might be a little like this on one of those famous airships.

Madame Lefoux was standing before a vanity, putting the finishing touches to her toilette.

No one was helping her dress.

No one, it seemed, was needed.

She looked wonderful. She'd done something to her dark hair to make it even more glossy. She wore a suit perfectly tailored to her figure, with no attempt to hide any femininity. True, she was slender, but Imogene still found that figure very finely curved indeed. Madame Lefoux's trousers and frock coat were soft blue, and her waistcoat a black paisley over silver with touches of the same blue. She wore a black cravat that made her eyes appear enormous and her skin very white.

She turned to find Imogene gawping.

"Oh, good, Miss Hale." She seemed to have recovered her cool aplomb. "This pin is quite fiddly, would you mind?"

Imogene didn't mind in the least.

The inventor smelled mostly of vanilla with only the tiniest lingering hint of machine oil and coal smoke. Imogene tried to slow her excited breathing as she stood, so near, and concentrated on threading the pin through the inventor's neck tie without damaging any of the fine silk. The pin was a simple silver filigree with one small blue center stone. Nevertheless, it looked expensive. *Could inventors afford sapphires? Was this a gift from some former patron? Or lover?*

"Careful, it is loaded."

Which is when Imogene realized it was a dart emitter of some kind. Was the inventor expecting trouble this evening?

"What with?" Imogene asked, trying to sound timid.

"Numbing agent. Not effective in the long term on supernaturals, but works a treat for a good ten minutes or so."

I thought she was friendly with the London Pack. Or is it the vampires she's worried about? Imogene dared not ask. She didn't want to push her luck, standing too close, breathing in the other woman's scent. The last thing she wanted was the inventor leaping away from her again. *I don't think my pride could take it.*

Imogene was pleased to find that her fingers shook only slightly, and Madame Lefoux didn't seem to notice. Or if she did, she attributed it to the danger inherent in a loaded cravat pin and not the inexplicable urge to stroke the neck underneath.

"Thank you, Miss Hale." She had gone all stiff and reserved again.

Imogene drew away, crestfallen. "Dr Caedes says you're wanted in the drawing room. Lady Maccon was asking after you."

The inventor brightened. "Was she? Good. But I believe I shall make her wait a little longer. After all, she put me in this position – she can suffer the dubious company of Caedes and Hematol for a while longer. Let her stew."

Imogene only nodded. "May I be of assistance with anything else?"

The inventor touched her cheek. "Thank you, *choupinette*, no."

Was it wishful thinking or had her hand trembled a little? Perhaps she was thinking of Lady Maccon.

Imogene turned to leave.

"What *really* happened to your ankle?" The inventor's tone was sharp, almost angry.

"Nothing, Madame, an accident."

"Oh, indeed?" Madame Lefoux did not sound convinced.

Imogene turned back to her, fearful. "Please don't concern yourself."

The green eyes narrowed. "I do not have time this evening, but we *will* discuss this further."

Imogene sighed and gave a little nod.

"Ridiculous British stiff-upper-lipping," muttered the inventor.

Imogene gimped back downstairs in a fog. How could Madame Lefoux be so many things at once? Kind and encouraging, cool and polite, and then angry and concerned? Imogene didn't know what to do or how to react. *How can I flirt when she won't stick to one mood longer than three seconds? Clearly, she's affected by me, but what good if I cannot control the effect?* Imogene's needs were simple. She wanted the inventor to want her. Yet Madame Lefoux seemed bent upon every feeling *but* wanting.

The butler was still puttering outside the drawing room when Imogene returned.

"Well, is she coming?"

"Soon, I think."

"She's punishing the Maccons, I suppose."

Imogene gave him a dignified look.

The butler acknowledged her silence as a respectful reprimand for his nosiness. "Quite right. Best not involve ourselves."

Imogene reentered the room.

The atmosphere was tense and the request for Madame Lefoux's presence seemed to have been forgotten.

Lord Maccon was standing and yelling at the Duke of Hematol about something political.

Lady Maccon was frowning furiously at her husband and instructing him to "Sit down, for goodness' sake. No one is impressed with your ridiculous posturing."

Dr Caedes was wringing his hands, or at least the vampire equivalent, which meant he was showing fang and drooling slightly.

Major Channing seemed to be finding the whole

thing very funny indeed. He was leaning back in his chair with arms crossed over his chest and a supercilious expression.

"You've redecorated the room again, haven't you?" Lady Maccon said to Dr Caedes, somewhat desperately.

"The countess enjoys new curtains every season."

Lady Maccon raised her eyebrow. "What a novel affectation."

Imogene took up position near the door, awaiting the tea trolley. She watched Lady Maccon intently. What was she to Madame Lefoux?

Lady Maccon was a substantial female. Everything about her was in excess – from bosom to nose to voice. And she was forthright about all of it, particularly the bosom. The combination was more than the drawing room could easily contain (although it was a large drawing room). She was also sufficiently rich and titled to say what she thought without consequence. Imogene respected that well enough, envied it slightly, but she didn't understand the basis of the appeal (aside from the bosom, of course).

Lord Maccon watched his wife (when he wasn't glaring at the duke) with eyes that fair shone with affection. So, he clearly understood. Major Channing, on the other hand (or should that be: on the other *paw*?) seemed to find Lady Maccon barely tolerable. The two vampires regarded her with something akin to fear.

Imogene found that confusing. What had

vampires to fear from a mere mortal? Even one as bossy as Lady Maccon? True, the bosoms were awe-inspiring, but it wasn't like she could smother a vampire with them. Vampires didn't breathe, did they?

When the door opened, Imogene assumed it would be the butler. But instead, Madame Lefoux entered the room.

"My dear Alexia!" she cried, sounding more than normally French. She swept across the floor to bow low, in a decidedly affected manner, and press an ardent kiss to Lady Maccon's proffered hand. For one brief moment, Imogene caught a flash of green eyes glancing at her. Madame Lefoux, at least, was well aware of Imogene's presence. She tried not to shiver from that quick look.

"Madame Lefoux, what a pleasure to see you at last." Lady Maccon grinned.

They're flirting! Imogene realized. *Right there in front of two werewolves and two vampires, and a handful of servants. And her husband! Flirting shamelessly!* This gave new weight to the bosoms.

"You look lovely this evening, Alexia. New dress? Did Biffy pick it out for you?"

"Of course. You know I cannot manage such things on my own."

The inventor turned. "Lord Maccon, a pleasure."

"Lefoux," growled the Alpha. There was no real heat to it. He, at least, felt no concern for his wife's virtue in the inventor's presence. *Foolish overconfidence,* wondered Imogene, *or does he know something I don't?*

"Was the train here a horrible bother?"

"Horrible," agreed Lady Maccon. "No tea at all, and the pace quite frantic. I'm sure it can't be good for the constitution."

"You are gloriously robust, Alexia. In a contest of wills between you and a steam engine, I should not wager on the steam engine."

"Coming from you, my dear, that's true flattery."

They were most definitely flirting. *Disgusting! With a married woman!*

Lord Maccon looked on indulgently.

Finally, Madame Lefoux moved on from the Maccons. "Major Channing? How unexpected."

The big blond inclined his head. "Madame Lefoux." His mouth was twisted in a slight sneer.

The inventor tuned back to Lord Maccon. "Interesting choice."

The Alpha glanced at his Gamma. "Sometimes, one must take him out into polite company for an airing. If only to see whether he's grown any manners in the interim."

"And if he must be brought out, why not inflict him upon vampires?" suggested Madame Lefoux, as if said vampires were not already in the room and bristling at being ignored.

"Exactly."

Lady Maccon interjected, "Who more deserving?"

Major Channing sniffed. "I *can* behave myself. Better than either of you, if the recent discussion is anything to go by."

Imogene felt oddly protective of him while

simultaneously afraid he might notice her and remark. Why were they picking on the poor man? He still hadn't recognized her. Or wasn't going to show recognition. Imogene knew herself to be beautiful, but that didn't make household staff any less part of the furniture. Right now, she was one more pretty thing the vampires had collected.

Madame Lefoux said, "Well, isn't this going to be a *delightful* evening? Now tell me, how is the infant-inconvenience?"

Lord Maccon instantly softened and began prattling on about his daughter. Imogene gathered that this was a child of some post-talking, pre-schooling age. There was mention of a guardian named Lord Akeldama, and of the child being somewhat gifted, or cursed, or encumbered by an excess of philosophy.

Imogene was left confused. Everyone knew neither vampires nor werewolves could breed. So, this daughter must be Lady Maccon's issue from a previous marriage. Kind of Lord Maccon to be so welcoming and loving towards the girl.

The tea and food were brought in, and the conversation flowed more freely as a result. Imogene followed very little of it as she glided about, serving canapés. Raw liver on tiny toast tips for the werewolves. Foreign grapes, imported at great expense, and aged cheddar for the ladies. The vampires, of course, ate nothing.

Instead of trying to understand the discussion itself, Imogene watched the flow of interest and control. Lord Maccon held the highest social position but was breezy about it. His wife was something significant as Dr Caedes occasionally referred to her, in an awkward way, as *muhjah*. This title appeared to confer with it considerable rank, possibly political in nature. Although Imogene had never heard of a woman who held power in government – aside from Queen Victoria, of course.

The two vampires, consequently, were forced to occupy the inferior social position, with Major Channing bringing up the rear. He was third tier in the London Pack, plus a major in the Coldsteam Guards, and as such accustomed to command. Lowest rank did not sit well, poor chap.

Thus the circling of the predators in the room (verbal though it might be) was fraught.

Madame Lefoux flitted through it all – more French, more erudite, more relaxed, and more charming than ever. She donned fine manners and big words as easily as she did a top hat. She did not glance in Imogene's direction again.

And she touched Lady Maccon a great deal more than was necessary.

Imogene was not to wait at table. As soon as the bell rang and the party adjourned to the dining room, she assumed her duties for the night were discharged.

One of the drones, however, stopped her in the hallway.

"Imogene, dear. Come with me."

"Miss Venables?"

Most of the hive drones were male, but occasionally Countess Nadasdy took a female. She had hopes of someday making another queen, no matter how slim the odds. There was always some poor woman who wished to try for immortality regardless of the extreme risk. Right now, that woman was Miss Abigail Venables.

Miss Venables was a harpist of renown. She had thick red hair, big brown eyes, and full lips. Imogene thought her wildly beautiful but awfully cold.

"What can I do for you, ma'am?" Imogene asked politely.

"Ah, no, it is for me to help you. We are of a similar size. You are to borrow one of my dresses for this evening." Miss Venables began walking away, assuming Imogene would follow.

Imogene followed. "I am?" Confusion cut through her. Why on earth would she need a dress?

"Yes, indeed, one of my best dinner gowns, with a very low neckline. Pity to waste it, but I'm sure she'll buy me another."

"I'm to *attend* the meal?" There could be no other explanation. "But I'm a parlourmaid!"

"No, dear, no. You are to *be* the meal."

CHAPTER FIVE

In Which Things Get Perverted at Supper

Imogene was terrified. This wasn't what she wanted!

It was always a gamble, with vampires, whether they took you to bed or to eat. Imogene had hoped for the former. Then she'd met Madame Lefoux and hoped for neither.

And now supper.

The table was beautifully set. There was to be a specially prepared five-course meal in the French style for Madame Lefoux, Lady Maccon, and the attending drones. The two werewolves had trenchers of meat set before them that was a representative sample of all the game currently available throughout the countryside. It was very fresh and quite excessive.

And the vampires?

Next to each knelt a drone on a hassock, neck well exposed for feeding. Except that the spot beside the countess was empty. Miss Venables led Imogene there and then took her own seat partway down.

Imogene knew she must be very pale. Her skin prickled. Her neck felt cold and horribly bare. The dress was ridiculously low-cut. She'd never worn anything so fine (or so lacking in material) in her life.

It was fitted close to the full length of her body except for a great pouf of bustle out the back. It crinkled when she moved. Prey should never be allowed silence. It was white silk with a little jacket instead of sleeves that Miss Venables removed with ostentatious care right after they entered the room.

Imogene's arms and shoulders were now entirely bare. Her neck and chest were exposed in a way only streetwalkers, or *very* fine ladies, were ever allowed.

Imogene was humiliated. It was as if she were in her underpinnings!

Oh, they noticed her now. They *all* noticed her.

She looked up through her lashes.

Major Channing was grinning like a fool. He'd recognized her at last and no doubt thought it sweet that she'd found her way to the hive. A place of perversion for the perverted girl that only he'd ever noticed.

Lord and Lady Maccon seemed more uncomfortable than anything else. Perhaps it was the nature of her dress, or perhaps it was the vampires' feeding style that disconcerted the couple. Werewolves could be prudish about other supernaturals.

Dr Caedes looked both annoyed and hungry. His eyes were fixed on Imogene's chest. Lord Ambrose's brooding was disturbed by a slight interest. Imogene felt a twinge of pride; he ordinarily showed concern for nothing beyond the queen's safety. Even the Duke of Hematol's reserved nature was shrouded with glittering avarice.

And Madame Lefoux?

Imogene couldn't bear to look at her. It was too awful. This felt like a betrayal. As if the inventor had staked a claim and been denied, and now it was being rubbed in her face. Imogene was being used by the vampires to inflict pain on the only person there she cared anything about.

Look, the vampires were saying. *She is ours, not yours.*

Imogene wanted to scream that she belonged to no one. They had no right, no right at all!

Except perhaps they did. They were her masters, after all. And they were vampires. And she'd known when she took work with them that this complicated matters. She had counted on it.

It didn't help that she was out of her depth – wearing a dress that wasn't hers, standing in a place of honor that she'd not earned, amongst company entirely beyond her station.

Madame Lefoux had tried to handle everything quietly. She'd asked for nothing more than a little extra help in the laboratory, with no mention of Imogene's skill with numbers. Or her beauty. And now Imogene was standing before them all like some anointed offering. She'd become a prize over which they would bicker, a way of punishing the inventor for some unnamed crime. Perhaps the crime of asking for what she needed. Or the crime of not wanting to be at the hive. Or the crime of noticing a servant and showing her favor.

Imogene felt ridiculous, and unworthy, stuffed into that too-small, too-beautiful gown. She was afraid to move for fear she would spill out or split a seam. The stays (also on loan from Miss Venables) were stiffer than her working corset and designed to show the drape of a dress rather than to permit any freedom of movement.

Imogene was angry that it must be done this way. She'd known all along what might be her fate in a vampire hive, but she'd believed they'd be circumspect. After all, this was her first time! Weren't vampires lauded for their discretion?

Her eyes burned, but she knelt, waiting. There was no point in running; they were all stronger and faster, supernaturally so. And they were all predators by nature; should she flee, even the werewolves would give chase.

She had ignored all the warnings.

She had sleepwalked long enough.

"Is she not stunning?" The countess stroked Imogene's naked arm from bicep to wrist, tracing the blue veins visible there.

Imogene shivered.

"I've been keeping her for a special occasion. Waiting for her to ripen. Such a reserved young thing. One wouldn't think, with such beauty, that she'd be so meek. But some underlings never learn, do they? Ridiculous to think they can be taught anything. I don't know why Snodgrove keeps going on about educating the masses. You wouldn't want that, would you, sweet thing?"

Imogene would've answered but it wasn't really a question.

The queen kept stroking. "Of course you wouldn't. It's our sacred duty to speak for them. Poor,

weak little creatures. We know what's best for you."
She turned her attention to the table. "Is everyone
served? Shall we begin?"

The other three bare-necked drones immediately
tilted their heads invitingly.

Imogene did not. A small defiance. Also, her
thighs were shaking. She felt if she tried to move,
she'd fall over.

The queen yanked on her wrist, hard, pulling her
to the side.

Instinctively, she jerked away, overbalanced, and
crashed forward. Her chin struck the table edge hard,
knocking her teeth together and jarring her neck. She
saw stars.

The crack was loud in the silence.

Everyone waited.

The queen smiled, big and broad and showing *all*
her fangs. The smile didn't reach her eyes. They were
colder and harder than the grip around Imogene's
wrist.

Imogene righted herself with effort but didn't tilt
her head. Instead, she hung it, staring down at the
tabletop.

Out of the corner of her eye she saw Countess
Nadasdy tilt hers instead – a query or a defiance or an
acknowledgment? Imogene couldn't read vampire
body language.

"Very good. Dinner is served."

The male vampires bent, clamped mouths to necks,
and began to feed. A soft rhythmic slurping permeated

the air.

Imogene couldn't see much from her humbled position, but she had to assume, from the gnawing noises, that the two werewolves were eating as well.

Countess Nadasdy dropped Imogene's wrist to grab her hair, yanking her head to one side.

Imogene's chin ached and the stars returned, spearing a shaft of pain through her head. She swallowed convulsively.

"Delightful," said the vampire queen.

The sound of something being slammed onto the table reverberated around the room.

"Enough!"

A chair scraped. Light, assertive footsteps approached.

Imogene found herself pulled to her feet, gentle hands on her shoulders, and then guided to stand behind Madame Lefoux's slender form. The inventor was now between her and the vampire queen.

"How rude," said Countess Nadasdy, "disturbing my meal."

Everyone stopped eating and stared. The three male vampires looked almost comical, blood dripping from their fangs.

"Oh, isn't this charming! Are you volunteering in her place?"

At that moment, Imogene realized she was a pawn in a game she didn't understand.

Someone else stood at that statement. Lady Maccon. "Careful, Countess. You hold Genevieve's indenture, not her life. Blood was never in play."

The vampire queen looked sulky.

"You are only doing this because I asked for her!" Madame Lefoux's frustration was evident. Then, in a desperate attempt to explain to the avidly listening company, she said, "I wanted Miss Hale to assist in my work. I had come to rely more heavily on Quesnel than I realized. With him gone, my progress has slowed. But apparently, the duties of a parlourmaid take priority. My request was denied."

"You may not be entirely mine, inventor," said the countess on a hiss, "but *she is*!"

Imogene gritted her teeth. She was still feeling a mite dizzy, but she quite objected to that. She was a servant, not a slave!

"It is my legal right to take sustenance from my staff." Countess Nadasdy appealed to her guests.

"Only if they are willing." Lord Maccon's his deep voice was calm. "And only if you have exhausted your regular supply."

Imogene tried to put a respectful distance between herself and the inventor.

Madame Lefoux twisted her head slightly and whispered, "No, stay close. Safer that way." Her voice was warm, kind.

So, Imogene shifted to press against the inventor's back. It was firm beneath the coat. She fought not to nestle against the other woman, breathe in the scent of vanilla.

The countess shrugged. "We've had a busy evening. And as you can see, we only have three drones available for feeding. The others have already served for the night."

"Hungry, were we?" That was Major Channing,

an antagonizing sneer to his voice.

"Oh, for goodness' sake," said the vampire queen. "I want my supper, and it's incalculably rude to discuss the food in front of the food!"

"I will pay for her indenture." That was Madame Lefoux.

"Impossible!" spat Lord Ambrose.

"Alexia?" Madame Lefoux appealed to her friend for help.

Lady Maccon looked at her husband, eyebrow raised.

The Alpha shrugged. "He's right. Someone under indenture may not purchase an indenture herself. And we're all neglecting the fact that even if it were possible, the young lady would have to be willing." He inclined his shaggy head in Imogene's direction.

Imogene wished the floor would open up and swallow her whole. Everyone was staring at her now. Everyone was wondering why she was so special. She was disturbing their meal for no apparent reason. And all this while barely wearing any clothing on her upper half.

This has to be some kind of nightmare.

Henry was waiting at table; both first footmen were. They were staring too. None of the quality noticed that the staff was equally intrigued by this drama. Even the butler was mesmerized.

"Then let us settle this," said Lady Maccon. From her appearance, Imogene surmised that she was not the kind of woman who liked to be interrupted at mealtime. "I shall buy her indenture and loan her to Genevieve as a laboratory assistant."

"You cannot simply misappropriate my parlourmaid!" objected Countess Nadasdy.

"Oh, I think you'll find she can," said Lord Maccon, mildly. "So long as the lass agrees."

"Oh, good." Lady Maccon sat back down, satisfied. "Can we eat, then? I'm afraid, Countess, you'll have to find someone else to dust. Genevieve, if you'd see to your new assistant? Then we can get on."

Madame Lefoux turned to Imogene. "Miss Hale? What do you think?"

"I would be working with you? No one else? Forever?" It sounded like heaven.

The dimples appeared. "Not forever. An indenture is for a prescribed amount of time. Three years, for example."

"How long is yours?" Imogene felt emboldened enough to ask. Although she did so in a whisper, still conscious of how ridiculous she must look all gussied up in that low-cut dress.

"Ten, but I have already served four." Madame Lefoux gave a green-eyed look sideways at the countess. Then, seeming to sense Imogene's discomfort (or perhaps to further her point with the vampire queen), the inventor took one of Imogene's hands in a reassuring manner.

It was reassuring; it was also quite thrilling. Imogene squeezed and was delighted to get a squeeze in response.

Fortified by the support, she took a short breath and turned to face Lady Maccon. Imogene had thought this woman her rival, and yet she'd found her an unexpectedly stalwart ally. "I would ask for six years then, Muhjah." The title, which she'd only heard used once or twice, seemed appropriate.

Lady Maccon was clearly pleased with this request. Her eyes flicked back and forth between them. Taking in the clasped hands, they crinkled with delight. "Excellent! I'll have the articles drawn up at once. In the meantime, would you like to return with me to the pack house this evening?" She glared at Countess Nadasdy. "For the sake of your health."

Imogene felt another squeeze. "No, thank you, Muhjah. My understanding of vampires is that they'll obey the letter of the law, particularly if it's a law they helped to enact. That's assuming the articles take effect immediately, without my having signed anything."

Lord Maccon said, "Smart girl. Yes, they do. Supernatural or no, this is still England. We have always honored verbal contracts, and a woman's word is her bond. That, funnily enough, is also is a law that originated with the vampires."

Countess Nadasdy hissed in displeasure.

Lady Maccon said promptly, "My word on this."

Imogene replied timidly, "And mine."

"Bond observed," said Lord Maccon and Major Channing at the same time.

"Good." Lady Maccon's tone turned pitiful. "May we please eat now? I'm starving."

Madame Lefoux did not let go Imogene's hand, instead using it to lead her from the room.

Safely out in the hallway, the inventor let out a long, shaky breath. Her eyes, focused on Imogene, were almost hungry with worry.

Imogene rubbed her aching chin with her free hand.

"Oh, your poor face. And that limp earlier. You've had a rough time of it, *choupinette*. I am so very sorry. My attention has done you more harm than good, and it was misinterpreted. And now this."

Imogene tried to smile, but it hurt too much. "Best possible outcome. I much prefer to be your assistant than a parlourmaid."

"It is your own fault. Too beautiful by half. They were bound to make a centerpiece of you."

"I didn't do anything for it. For this." Imogene, frustrated, waved at her own body with one hand. Madame Lefoux still held the other. (Which was just about the best thing ever! *And she thinks I'm beautiful.*) "It's caused me nothing but grief."

"This is true. You do not seem to use beauty as a weapon, in the way of some I have known. It is… refreshing." Madame Lefoux's face fell, and, horribly, she dropped Imogene's hand and looked away.

She would become distant again now.

Imogene came over tense and sad, frustrated at having been set as a display, and a lesson, and a pawn, with no one caring for her feelings in the slightest. And frustrated that this sweet, courageous woman blew hot and then cold with such frequency.

Madame Lefoux was so close.

Imogene wanted so badly to feel embodied, to feel the sting of a reality where she wasn't cast adrift on the whims of those more powerful than herself.

Perhaps that was what drove her out of her sleepwalking daze into motion. Or was it gratitude for the rescue? Or was she merely responding to the squeeze of that hand in hers, a reassurance when she needed it most? Or maybe it was simply those hungry green eyes.

Whatever drove Imogene, it pushed her hard enough to overcome the stuffed-down fear of discovery, the up-tilted arrogance of protection. Imogene leaned forward and kissed the inventor. Another woman. For the very first time. Full on the mouth.

Madame Lefoux tasted of the wine she'd been sipping at supper. She smelled of vanilla, warm and buttery. And she leaned in towards Imogene, responding.

Her lips parted on a light breath of shock. They were so very, very soft.

Imogene wondered where to put her hands, and settled on the small of the other woman's back.

Then the inventor was no longer responding. And then she was gone, stepping back and out of reach.

"Imogene no, you do not have to express gratitude in such a way. I know it is not your…" She trailed off and ran a hand though her hair. It stuck a bit. She grimaced. "I hate pomade."

Imogene hung her head. "But I thought…" *You liked me. You fought for me because of something more than just arithmetic. Stupid Imogene. Foolish girl. To think yourself in any way worthy of such a woman as this. Her passion for her work. It is only the sums you do that appeal.*

"I would never want you to twist yourself to my desire. I need hardly say now that the rumors are true. But I have never taken an unwilling woman to my bed and I never shall."

But I'm willing! How else do I show you how willing?

"That's not it a'tall!" Imogene protested.

The inventor wouldn't listen. "This has been a horrid evening. You are hurt, embarrassed, and inappropriately dressed. You are grateful to me for saving you from worse, but I do not want you to offer yourself out of a sense of obligation."

She's being all noble. How very annoying. "But it's not…"

The dining room door opened and Lady Maccon's well-coiffed head stuck out. "Come back, Genevieve. It's perishing dull without you. Oh, send the poor girl to rest, do. She looks like death warmed over."

Madame Lefoux nodded. "Collect your things, Miss Hale. I'll have a cot arranged in my dressing room. You can sleep there."

Like a proper lady's maid, thought Imogene, thrilled and delighted by the implication. "Shall I be helping you dress, then?"

Madame Lefoux's mouth twitched. "Stop that."

Lady Maccon was listening, a broad grin on her face. "I can see why you like this one. She's more plucky than the quiet exterior would imply, isn't she?"

"And good with sums," insisted Madame Lefoux, holding the party line.

Lady Maccon's eyebrows went back up. "Is she,

now? Well, I'm sure that is the *entire* basis of her appeal. Now come along, do."

Madame Lefoux shook her head in mock exasperation and obeyed.

Imogene went to get her things and move into the dressing room.

Imogene settled into her new abode quickly (the dressing room was remarkably spacious – for a dressing room) and might have gone to sleep, but she was struck by the fact that she'd been discourteous to Lady Maccon.

I forgot to thank her! And I must tell her that I cannot sign the articles. Imogene couldn't write her own name, so she needed to make certain there was a way to still codify the indenture. She didn't want anything to stop her from taking this new path. To be tied to Madame Lefoux for six whole years. To work with numbers and engines. No dusting at all. Well, maybe a little dusting. And possibly some tidying. Would Madame Lefoux let her organize the laboratory? Imogene liked organization.

Regardless, it would be glorious. And she owed Lady Maccon everything.

I misjudged her horribly.

So, Imogene retrieved her parlourmaid's outfit from Miss Venable's room and dressed in it one final time. She still had her favorite duster, the brown-and-white, overly fluffy one that looked like Skoot (and had caused him to go barking mad with apparent jealousy the one time she waved it at him). She wondered if Skoot could come visit the potting shed regularly. And if she might keep the duster.

Thus disguised as her former self, Imogene made her way partly down the main stairs. She found a nice hiding spot on the landing, in a shadowed corner, behind one of the more modern statues. (The one she thought looked like a concerned bipedal potato with stomach troubles.) She could watch the dining room door from there and maybe catch the muhjah before she departed.

How not to make a scene of it? That was the real question.

As it happened, Imogene was presented with an excellent opportunity directly after supper, although not quite in the way she'd expected.

Vampires still observed segregation once a meal concluded (although this was considered horribly old-fashioned by most). Thus Imogene witnessed the ladies heading for the drawing room.

Countess Nadasdy led the way, still vibrating in annoyance. Or perhaps this was a new annoyance that had nothing to do with Imogene. Miss Venables followed close on her heels. Lady Maccon and Madame Lefoux, the only other ladies present, brought up the rear. They held back at the base of the stairs, directly below Imogene's hiding spot, clearly eager for a private word.

Imogene couldn't help herself. She cupped her ear to listen.

"A parlourmaid who does sums. Extraordinary."

Imogene blushed to realize that they were talking about *her!*

Lady Maccon's bosom heaved in mock annoyance. "What is it with you and maids, Genevieve? I mean to say, really."

"It is those little black dresses, darling." The inventor was back to flirting.

Imogene was back to being upset by their evident affection. Lady Maccon was nice and all, but did she have to be so overt about it? Imogene pursed her lips. She tried to believe that while flirting was clearly a cornerstone of their relationship, there didn't seem to be any follow-through. Unless Lord Maccon was a great deal less possessive than any other werewolf *ever*.

Madame Lefoux continued, "But seriously now, she is not for me."

Lady Maccon was having none of it. "And how do you know that?"

"Look at her. So young and innocent, so beautiful. So ripe for some man to pluck."

"Don't be crude, dear. How do you know she doesn't want a more delicate sort of plucking?"

"*You* never did."

"I never knew to ask. It was too late, anyway."

"You could run away with me now." The inventor made a dramatic flail in the direction of the front door.

Lady Maccon rolled her eyes so hard, Imogene swore she could hear it from her hiding spot. "Do be serious for one moment. I *like* her."

"How could you possibly form an opinion? She barely strings six words together."

"Exactly. My world could use a few more strong,

silent people."

"Alexia…"

"Well, I *do* like her! She watches you. She looks at you the way Conall looks at me."

"Does she indeed?"

"You never noticed?"

"You are willfully misinterpreting hero worship, I fear. She has a brilliant mind. Untrained, of course. Not schooling the peasant stock is truly a sin against science."

"Oh, I see. Your interest in the girl is purely intellectual." Any more sarcasm and Lady Maccon's voice would strip wallpaper.

"She is half my age!"

"Not quite."

"How would you know?"

Lady Maccon planted her hands on her generous hips. "What are you so afraid of, Genevieve?"

The inventor's voice became tired and muted. "Of it happening all over again. Of losing again. As I lost Angelique. As I lost you."

"You never lost me."

"Yes. I did."

"Don't be silly, you never had me to begin with."

"Fair point."

Imogene peeked around her gastric-potato-guardian statue. The gaslights in the hallway were low and sputtering. Under the shifting shadows, the inventor's face was sharp and drawn, almost haggard.

"I cannot go through it all again, Alexia."

Lady Maccon nodded, equally serious. Her face was almost handsomely grave in the low light. "I know, dear. I know. But it would be worse, don't you think, to never try at all? Aren't you lonely? Especially now Quesnel is at university."

The inventor bit her lip and winced. "Horribly. You stranded me in the middle of nowhere. Essex, for goodness' sake! It is not civilized. I barely even have my inventions."

"Yes, and I am sorry for it, and for you. Although that is *not* an apology! You deserved worse and we both know it. You destroyed half of London. And you're French. That simply cannot be ignored or glossed over. What else was I to do?"

"I loathe it when you are reasonable."

"Everyone says that." Lady Maccon put a hand to her friend's arm, drawing her close.

Imogene tensed.

"See here, Genevieve, I shouldn't have to tell you this. But you rendered me a great service once." At some nonverbal cue, Lady Maccon added, "Very well, more than once, and I shall now attempt to return the favor with good advice." She paused dramatically. "Try to make it better for yourself. You are stuck here for *six more years*. And if you cannot do it for yourself, make it better for that poor pining girl. I've given you the means."

Imogene straightened, embarrassed that her yearning had shown so clearly to a stranger.

Madame Lefoux was frustrated. "Miss Hale is suffering under a warped sense of obligation. I do not believe she is *inclined*, not really."

"Tempting her into a ladies' pew, are you? Well, that's not my area of expertise. I will bow to your experience in identifying..." Lady Maccon floundered. "Other ladies' ladies, as it were. But, Genevieve, and I mean this seriously—"

"Yes, Alexia?"

"Don't botch it."

"Yes, Alexia."

"No octopuses."

"Yes, Alexia. I mean, no, Alexia. I mean, whatever you say, Alexia."

"Good, now let's suffer through the last of this ghastly evening together and then you can go see to your girl."

"She is not *my* girl!"

"Whatever you say, Genevieve."

CHAPTER SIX

In Which Imogene Contemplates Rodger

Imogene never got her chance to thank Lady Maccon.

Fortunately, when the articles of indenture arrived by aetherogram, Madame Lefoux said an X would do for a signature. Thus everything became legally binding seamlessly. The vampires couldn't complain; they had written the law to make it easy in the first place.

It heralded a glorious new life for Imogene, that of *laboratory assistant and,* Madame Lefoux insisted on adding, *chief finder of the elusive x.*

Imogene took to the equations with renewed vigor and learned the names of all Madame Lefoux's tools, and those of the engines and engine parts. She took over shoveling coal and keeping the burners at exactly the correct temperature.

Lady Maccon sent along a half-dozen durable working dresses (from London!) and Madame Lefoux found Imogene a spare leather apron. Imogene need

never again dress as a parlourmaid. (Unless Madame
Lefoux really did have a thing for little black dresses?)
She kept one service outfit, just in case, and passed
the rest on to her family, whose circumstances were
also improved by her new position. Lady Maccon was
more than generous with Imogene's salary, and with
the inventor providing meals, she needed very little.
Madame Lefoux even tentatively offered to order
Imogene some trousers, but Imogene felt that would
be taking things too far.

Already she must avoid all contact with Henry
and the other members of staff. Most of them felt she
had betrayed them. The rest felt she was reaching
above her station. Trousers might tip everyone into
madness. Trousers were a powerful weapon of chaos,
if Madame Lefoux was anything to go by.

Imogene took tea and luncheon via tray in the
shed alongside her inventor, but for the evening meal,
she still must join the servants, butler presiding. The
butler clearly believed she was getting above herself.
Thus, he overlooked any pettiness at table with
regards to food dropped on Imogene's new dress, or
not passing the butter, or what have you.

But that was only one of two blights on
Imogene's otherwise idyllic new life as laboratory
assistant (and chief finder of the elusive x). The other
blight was Madame Lefoux herself.

Imogene tried several more times to encourage
the inventor's physical interest, but her tentative
touches and expressions of affection were rebuffed.
She garnered the occasional dimpled smile and
sometimes (perhaps it was wishful thinking) a quick,

hungry green-eyed glance, but nothing more. She was at a loss how to convince Madame Lefoux that her affection was genuine without it being misconstrued as gratitude. Not that she wasn't grateful. She *loved* the assistant job. She always found the x no matter how elusive. She was far better at it than she ever had been as a parlourmaid. (And frankly, she'd been a good parlourmaid, which made her an *excellent* laboratory assistant. *And the x? The x is mine!*)

How to tell the inventor that it wasn't gratitude leaving Imogene aching and restless each night? (Nor was it coal shoveling – not that kind of ache.) It wasn't gratitude turning her cold and lonely in her cot, although it was more generous a bed than she'd ever had before. Madame Lefoux had provided soft quilts and a *down* mattress. Imogene could hardly believe it. *Down!*

Imogene spent her nights wishing beyond anything that she might leave that feathered luxury and lie next to her new mistress instead. They would not even have to *do* anything. Not unless Madame Lefoux wanted to. It would be magic simply to curl up with her.

Imogene lacked the vocabulary to say anything. Her few stuttering tries were dismissed out of hand. The inventor was remarkably stubborn. She was determined to believe Imogene incapable of genuine interest. And Imogene was at a loss as to why. Who on earth *wouldn't* be interested in Genevieve Lefoux? *Curses.*

How could Madame Lefoux still think that Imogene preferred men? Or was it something else?

Perhaps she genuinely believed Imogene too innocent. *And whose fault is that? I have tried. No one seems to want to make me less so.*

The inventor had responded to their kiss so it couldn't be dislike. *Could it?* Maybe she hadn't really responded. Maybe she'd simply been kind, trying not to react in horror or disgust to Imogene's bumbling advances. *Maybe I'm not the kind of girl she desires.*

There was the conversation in the hallway with Lady Maccon to consider. Madame Lefoux, who seemed so fearless, was frightened of something. Lady Maccon said so. So, maybe it wasn't Imogene at all but despair holding the inventor in check.

Perhaps I should just strip bare and climb under her counterpane.

"Dear Genevieve," she imagined herself saying (she was far more direct and confident in her fantasies). *Genevieve* was what Lady Maccon called Madame Lefoux, and it was such a perfect name. Imogene called her Genevieve a lot – in her head.

"Dear Genevieve," she would say, "I love that you are full of finer feelings and insist upon protecting me from myself, but if you do not rodger me this instant, I may perish away for the lack."

Although, did two ladies together call it *rodgering*? Or was there a proper, more feminine word? *Gertruding,* perhaps?

You see! Not only do I need her physically, I need her to teach me how to even talk about such things. Let alone do them. For surely Genevieve was experienced in such matters.

I certainly hope so. One of us should know what

she is about.

Overly optimistic, that. For while Imogene lay awake and aching, hungry for something she couldn't name, the inventor continued blithely on about her inventing as if nothing had altered. And while Madame Lefoux did indeed insist that Imogene get *an education,* that education didn't extend beyond the realm of laboratory sciences, mathematics, reading, and writing.

More's the bloody pity, thought Imogene, frustrated beyond measure. They were together *all the time* now.

It was wonderful.

And it was *utter torture.*

Imogene liked the learning. In the space of only a few months, she'd mastered the basics of reading and writing. She couldn't spell worth crackling, but she didn't need that for equations.

And the equations were glorious! Nothing was more fun than solving for x. It was like the most perfect of quests. Imogene felt herself to be a white knight, and the x her dragon to find and slay.

Although, to be honest, Imogene did believe there was something more fun, something involving Genevieve and her dimples and her other bits, but for now she must settle for slaying the x.

Summer wended into fall, and Imogene managed to keep to the potting shed and gardens except for the evening meal. Skoot made his way to her at least half the time. The white of his fur took on a grey dusting of soot and he was prone to sneezing, but he seemed to very much enjoy the laboratory's range of sounds, smells, and activity. Madame Lefoux didn't object to his presence. Once or twice, Imogene even caught her chatting to the little dog in French.

"He is a Papillon, so he must understand his native tongue, no?" the inventor explained at Imogene's grin.

"Naturally."

Genevieve looked away quickly at that, as if hurt by Imogene's enthusiasm.

The lunch tray began to include a bit of chopped liver in a little saucer.

Lacking any other options, Imogene continued to eat supper with the household. She wasn't staff anymore. As an indenture, she ranked higher, not quite a drone but no longer a servant. But the drones never invited her to join them, and she didn't know how to ask. It was all rather awkward.

She felt it too petty a matter to mention to Genevieve. The inventor had other concerns.

Madame Lefoux was required to present herself to the hive for the sunset repast (their breakfast, her supper) and report on her latest endeavors. Imogene was mildly afraid that if she said anything about her awkward mealtimes, she'd be forced to join the vampires at table. The inventor had odd ideas about equality and believed Imogene's standing almost on par with her own. Imogene would suffer the butler's disregard, Henry's hostility, and the staff's animosity if it meant no vampires. Perhaps they would forget about her. Perhaps everyone would forget about her.

They did not.

"I'll be leaving tomorrow, Miss Hale."

Imogene blinked up from her current set of calculations. Her breath caught and her stomach clenched, but she tried not to let it show. "Oh. Will you, Madame? Not for too long, I hope?"

"Ah, sweet *choupinette*. Only a week or so. I am off to meet my son in London. He needs new clothes again. Boys will keep growing. He's coming over on the trans-Channel dirigible so we can visit Bond Street. I thought I'd present that paper the Royal Society has been prodding me about. You know, the one on the counterstate aetheric conductor? I would ask you along, but those catchment reductions must be monitored. I do not trust anyone else while I am away."

Imogene smiled. Wasn't it just like Genevieve to even consider inviting her? She'd never been to London; it seemed a terrifying place. "And who would keep an eye on Skoot? Regardless, I wouldn't want to impose on your time with your son. I know you miss him." Plus, she was honored the inventor trusted her with the laboratory while she was away.

Madame Lefoux moved close to her then.

Imogene's breathing stuttered. Usually Genevieve was fastidious in her avoidance of all contact between them.

Elegant callused hands touched her cheek, trembling and tentative. "Please stay safe while I'm gone? Be careful."

Imogene tried not to breathe, afraid she might startle the inventor as one would a wild creature. "I will," she whispered.

And the hand was gone, as was Genevieve. Withdrawing again. *Withdrawing like always!* Imogene suppressed a growl of frustration.

And Imogene was left alone in the hive house.

She was as careful as promised, but some patterns had been set into place that put her at risk. Henry, for example, was back to bringing out the trays for meals. Also, Cook expressed her displeasure at Imogene's new status by limiting those meals to stewed tea, weak and without milk, and a chunk of stale bread. Similarly, her luncheon devolved to servant's stew or porridge – not that Imogene was inclined to complain, but it was a statement.

It began the very first day. Henry slapped down the tray with no concern for Imogene's calculations, spilling all over the most recent set. Imogene had more care to her papers than Madame Lefoux, and he'd ruined in one fell swoop all of yesterday's work.

He leaned over, his mouth fetid as old fish, pressing against her in the guise of looking over her work. As if he understood any of it.

"Thank you, Henry," she said, "You may go."

"So high and mighty now you've slept your way upstairs." He made a rude gesture with his tongue, leaning even closer.

Imogene could feel his hot breath on her neck.

"Lots of work, is it, sweetheart? Lots of nighttime duties, keeping her satisfied?"

I wish, thought Imogene.

Then Henry licked her neck, one long swoop of clammy tongue.

Imogene crashed her chair back into him as she stood up, shoving herself away from the desk.

"Careful," said Henry, "Wouldn't want to spill anything further. Mess up more of these important scribbles of yours."

Imogene poured the hot tea over his head.

Henry screamed. Two of the under-gardeners and Skoot came to see what was going on.

Skoot went into yapping, bouncing hysterics.

"She's loony," Henry accused, pointing a finger. "Just dumped scalding tea all over me!" By which statement he neatly prevented himself from staying any longer.

The under-gardeners made no comment, leaving Imogene alone and shaking. Except for Skoot, of course. The act of calming him down helped Imogene. His little pink tongue on her cheek licked away the salt there.

She went into the house for luncheon and made it known to the cook that she'd prefer only one meal a day brought out, and please would she send someone other than Henry?

The cook was smug, thinking her introduction of weak tea responsible for a now-diminished workload. But she wouldn't concede that anyone other than Henry should play delivery boy. "None of my staff can be spared. It's his duty. Stop trying to meddle."

Later that day, Imogene noticed the inductive coupler was missing. She thought she'd placed it right there, next to the desk, but a search everywhere yielded no coupler.

"Where has it gone to?" she asked the wicker chicken.

The wicker chicken only loomed at her, menacing. It wasn't like Skoot to steal something. He wasn't that kind of dog.

Imogene had instituted, hesitantly, some level of organization to the potting shed. Madame Lefoux didn't object once she discovered that this meant her tools could be found more easily (surprise, surprise) and Imogene could respond more quickly to her requests. Imogene, now that she knew her letters, rather wished to alphabetize everything, but that was going too far.

And she wasn't allowed to move the wicker chicken.

"He has sentimental value," explained Madame Lefoux.

When Skoot was elsewhere, the chicken was company of a kind, Imogene supposed.

But the missing coupler worried her. It was made of pure copper, an expensive bit of kit, which made her suspicious.

The next day, when Henry brought her luncheon, he thrust her up against an engine pillion hard enough to bruise. Imogene screamed this time. Skoot bit Henry's ankle, and when the gardeners came to check on the fuss, Henry let her go.

A sheaf of Madame Lefoux's notes went missing.

The coupler might have been an aberration. It could be sold for scrap at a nice rate, so one might forgive its disappearance as opportunistic avarice. But notes were a different thing. Notes meant industrial espionage. Imogene knew that Genevieve had intellectual enemies. She was a brilliant inventor, and the hive would hold her patents. Many others wanted to profit from them instead – wanted it very badly indeed.

Imogene began leaving the laboratory at noon, locking it behind her, and waiting for her tray outside. This also put her in full view of the gardeners, who were reasonable chaps and beginning to suspect the nature of her and Henry's relationship. They wouldn't interfere, not really; the business of inside staff was to left to inside staff. Just as downstairs didn't involve themselves with upstairs. But Henry couldn't steal anything this way.

This technique worked for a few meals. Henry shoved the tray at her with nothing more than a curse, turned, and walked off. Imogene ate outside, and returned the tray to the kitchen herself.

Then, on the fifth day, she became distracted with a particularly delectable equation. She missed the arc of the sun and Henry had his excuse once more.

She took the hit to confirm her suspicions. The hit being her neck licked again and one crude grope in the vicinity of her left breast. She tossed her head back into his teeth. Which cut her head, but bloodied his lip – which was most satisfying.

He swore at her.

"I'll scream again," she warned.

"Eventually, they'll realize it happens every time I visit, and stop coming. Then where will your protectors be?"

He left then. Imogene was relatively certain she saw a roll of papers tucked under his vest.

Lacking any other option, Imogene took her concerns to the butler.

"He's stealing notes from the lab," she insisted, getting straight to the point.

"That's a serious accusation, young lady."

Imogene was militant. "Also a rather valuable tool. Copper, about so big, slightly squiggly."

"And what do you expect me to do about it?" The butler looked down his nose at her.

"Have his room searched, of course."

The butler twisted his mouth. "How do I know you aren't casting doubt on poor Henry because you can't handle the tasks Drone Lefoux left you to complete? You lose a tool, blame Henry. Not smart enough to finish your work, blame Henry. He makes for an excellent scapegoat for your incompetence. Don't think I haven't noticed there's bad blood between you."

"But he did it! All you have to do is search and find out. Unless he's already disposed of the evidence. If he's an industrial spy and you don't catch him, there'll be hell to pay from Madame Lefoux when she returns."

The butler only sniffed. "I think not. Henry is such a *nice* boy. Everyone likes him. I feel it more likely you're using him than that he's engaged in espionage. He came to us with excellent references and he's been with us much longer than you."

And that was that, so far as the butler was concerned.

Except that he must have mentioned something to Henry, because the first footman went out of his way to corner Imogene after supper.

He was very angry this time. No pretense at touching or even insults. It was the work of moments for him to slap her so hard across the face her cheek went numb.

Skoot was with his vampire masters, so she didn't even have her tiny fluffy knight.

Imogene tried to defend herself, but he slapped her again even harder, this time catching her eye with his fingernail.

Then one of the chambermaids walked in and Imogene fled to Genevieve's room.

Imogene was at a loss.

The problem of Henry and his abuse was one thing; she'd only a few more days to survive that, and then he would have to resort to more subtle meanness. Genevieve could be absent-minded when she was absorbed in her work, but she was an excellent guardian in her way. She was always aware of Imogene and watching out for her. Imogene caught her staring often, or casting little glances up at her while they worked. Henry would find it hard to touch her without the inventor noticing once said inventor returned.

But the stolen notes were a serious problem. Genevieve was very protective of her work, and Imogene was nothing if not loyal. In her own small way, she'd contributed to those notes on new gadgets, and papers on burgeoning aetherographic theory, and schematics for unusual devices. The very idea that they might be given to a competitor or sold on the open market to some lesser inventor was horrifying.

Where Imogene might not have had the courage to protest on behalf of her own safety, she felt compelled to take action when Genevieve's livelihood and reputation were at risk.

With no other option, she decided she must go over the butler's head and tell the hive of Henry's nefarious deeds. After all, this was their concern, their patents, and their responsibility to protect Genevieve's interests.

It being just after dark, and the shift changing from day to night, Imogene knew the vampires would be at breakfast. Countess Nadasdy always took hers in her room. Imogene couldn't think of anything else to do but go straight to the queen with her suspicions. The queen clearly saw some value in her, if only as a meal. Perhaps she would listen.

Despite the bad blood between her and Countess Nadasdy, or lack of blood as the case may be, the male vampires seemed a worse option. Dr Caedes was too sinister, always licking his lips when she passed him in the hallway. The Duke was too arrogant; he would dismiss her out of hand simply on the basis of her age, sex, and station. And Henry was a favorite with Lord Ambrose. That really only left her with the countess.

Imogene dressed in her Sunday best, still her nicest gown. Plus, it had a very high collar. She let her hair down, an extra barrier about her neck, and taking a deep breath, approached the queen's quarters.

Countess Nadasdy was already breakfasting when Imogene let herself in. The vampire queen was sitting up in bed, wearing a beautiful burgundy velvet dressing gown, with a pink damask tablecloth draped over her lap. On top of the cloth, one of the male drones was draped and arranged artfully. He was naked.

Imogene instantly turned to leave.

"Stay." Countess Nadasdy had seen her.

Of course she had. All the hive queen's senses were supernatural and advanced; it was impossible to sneak into the room of a vampire.

"I'm almost finished here." She bent her head back down and resumed a noisy sucking, after rotating the drone to a better angle, as if he were a pig on a spit.

Imogene tried not to look at the blood oozing from the first bite. She also tried not to look any further down the drone's body, as most of what he had was now facing her.

Imogene was a country-lass so she understood the mechanics of sex, most particularly the breeding of livestock. But she'd never had occasion to see a grown man without clothing before. Her younger brothers, of course, but this was different.

It's not a'tall nice-looking, she decided. And, in this instance, appeared recently well used. She wondered if the queen demanded other things from her drones before she ate.

Finally, the slurping stopped. Countess Nadasdy had finished her repast.

She patted her drone absently on his head and

later, as he crawled off the big bed, patted him on his bottom. Then she ignored him entirely.

"Come here, child."

Imogene came, stopping next to the bed but well out of grabbing distance.

"What has happened to your eye?" The queen's hair was a cascade of honey-brown curls about her face. They were awfully fluffy for a woman who was basically dead.

Imogene's face still smarted from Henry's attentions; she suspected the eye would be black and blue by morning. It must be an angry red at the moment.

"Henry, ma'am, the first footman."

The queen's eyes narrowed. "Well, you should inform your patron. It's her responsibility to protect you. You're *her* indenture, after all." It had never occurred to Imogene that an indenture incurred obligations of care on Lady Maccon's side. How on earth would she get a message to Lady Maccon? And over such a minor thing? The muhjah was such an important woman. No, Imogene refused to disturb her with her own trivial well-being. Still, it was nice to know she'd an alternative where she might report the spying, if the queen didn't cooperate.

"It's actually Henry I wished to discuss with you, ma'am."

The queen went stiff. "As I just said, it is not for me to interfere anymore. Remember, girl, *you* rejected *me*."

Imogene lowered her eyes, "I very much regret the incident." (Not a lie.) She jerked her chin up.

"Although the results seem positive. I believe I'm a good fit for the work, and I'm very much enjoying my new position."

"Oh, indeed? All the positions?"

"I'm sure I don't know what you mean."

"I'd be delighted to show you, pretty child. Feeding always makes me hungry for other, more carnal things."

A moan from the side of the room caused both human and vampire to remember that the male drone was still present. "And Beaumont here would love to join us. Wouldn't you, darling? Yes, I can see that you would."

Beaumont was still naked, so his interest was evident. *Just like with livestock.*

Imogene looked hurriedly away. "About Henry."

"Who is this Henry?"

"The first footman on the day shift, ma'am."

"Yes, well, I'm sure he looks the part, what else is there to consider?"

"I believe he's been stealing notes from the laboratory."

"Don't be ridiculous, girl. Why would the daytime first footman want your notes?"

"Not my notes, ma'am, Madame Lefoux's."

"Pah! I'm certain he was properly vetted. And it's *Drone* Lefoux"

"But they've gone missing and he's the only one with access to the potting shed, apart from me."

"You've likely misplaced them, then. Humans are so absent-minded. Or that tricky little inventor has. She will show you where they are when she returns."

"But I saw…"

"Enough!" In one of those movements that the human eye could barely follow, the vampire was on her feet. She had Imogene grasped tight, hard cold hands wrapped about her upper arms, holding her stiff and straight. Then Imogene found herself lifted up, so that her feet dangled in the air.

Countess Nadasdy might look smallish and roundish, and more akin to a barmaid than anything else, but she was unbelievably strong.

Then Imogene found herself flying through the air. The queen had tossed her, casually as a discarded muffin, onto the bed. She landed and bounced, scrabbling to get off as quickly as she could.

"No!" she said, loudly and firmly as the queen moved to follow her. And then, for good measure, "I do not want you."

Countess Nadasdy cocked her head, bird-like. "Who are *you* to reject *me*? Human insect. If I cannot bleed you, I shall bed you instead." The queen was on her and over her then, those cool hard hands wrapped about Imogene's hips, holding her down. If the vampire squeezed any more, she would surely shatter bone.

Somehow, Imogene remembered what had been said earlier. She remembered the fear in the vampires' eyes when they looked on the muhjah at that fateful supper party.

"I shall go to my patron." Imogene said, trying to keep her voice from trembling. "I shall tell Lady Maccon that you've abused me. I'm certain she is not the kind of woman to overlook such a thing. I may be a mere insect, but I'm *her* insect now. I'm not obligated to feed *any* of your hungers, ma'am, not even this one."

At that, the countess was off her and Imogene was up and running to the door.

"Do not visit me again in my chamber, girl," the queen called after her. "I will consider it evidence that you've changed your mind."

Imogene fled to Genevieve's room, closing the door firmly behind her. It too didn't have a lock, but the vampires respected Genevieve's territory. They had very strict protocols about such things. Imogene was pretty certain that, outside of a killing rage, none of them would come into Genevieve's room uninvited.

Hopefully, the countess was not in a killing rage.

Instinctively, Imogene dove not for her own bed, but for Genevieve's. She huddled there, under the heavy blankets, fully dressed, shaking as if in a bitter cold.

The pillow smelled of vanilla.

CHAPTER SEVEN

In Which We Learn the Source of Vanilla

A hand stroking her face woke Imogene.

The smell of vanilla was all around and she curled into the touch, responding to the calluses on those fingers, familiar friends, although she was not yet fully awake.

An amused voice said, "So, this is what you get up to when I am away? Staking a claim to the bigger bed, hum?"

Imogene sat up at once. Memory swept over her in a rush.

Genevieve Lefoux was sitting on the counterpane next to her, dressed for travel. A large hatbox and worn old carpetbag rested against the closed door behind her. She was smiling, but with Imogene upright, the dimples vanished.

"Why are you fully dressed?"

Gentle fingers coaxed Imogene's chin to move,

tilting her head into a beam of bright morning light.

The inventor's tone went icy. "Why is your eye black and your face bruised? What has happened, Imogene?"

Imogene, rather ridiculously, could only be thrilled by the use of her given name. Genevieve had never spoken it before with such intent. It was almost beautiful when colored with a French accent. An accent that was noticeably stronger at the moment.

"You're home early." *Thank heavens.*

"Imogene." The tone was very firm.

"It's a long story."

Genevieve's unbelievably gentle hand returned to sweep tangled hair out of Imogene's face.

I must look a fright. I never braided it to sleep. It's surely a bird's nest.

"I will not be angry. Well, not with you. Unless you slapped *yourself* in the face?"

Imogene bit her lip.

The inventor's hand didn't stop petting, capable fingers smoothing through Imogene's hair. "I find it best to begin at the beginning, *choupinette.*"

So, Imogene relayed the bare truth of what had happened. Henry and his hitting her, "Although that's not of real concern," she insisted. "What you must know is that he *stole* your notes. I haven't concrete proof, but two sets went missing. Each after one of Henry's visits. And I think he also lifted the inductive coupler."

"Hang the inductive coupler! I will see that little *fils de pute* drawn and quartered. I will guillotine his cock, I will…"

"I think he must be a spy," confessed Imogene, shaky. Hoping beyond hope that Genevieve, at least, would believe her.

"Of course he is a bloody spy! I only let him stay to keep an eye on him. And because he is so very *bad* at it. Stupid of me. I had no idea he would take it out on you. *Merde*. Why did you not tell me?" She paused, clearly putting a few mysteries to rest in her head. "That limp! He has been picking on you for a while. No?"

Much to Imogene's regret, the inventor stopped her caresses at that point.

Imogene ached with the lack. "Men don't like to be told no. But that isn't important. Didn't you hear, he *took your notes*? He could do real damage to your reputation."

"Blast my reputation!"

Imogene couldn't fail but be impressed by the dexterity with which Genevieve switched between swearing in French and English.

"How else has he hurt you, *choupinette*?"

Imogene couldn't hide the wince as she tried to get out of the bed. Her hips ached from the vampire queen's grip, as did her upper arms.

"No, don't move. You're better in my bed."

Imogene blinked at her, delighted.

"Oh, curses, you know what I mean."

Imogene felt she ought to confess all; Genevieve was bound to find out about her other injuries once she tried to move. "I went to the queen with my concerns."

Genevieve said something in French that was

likely very rude indeed; it was too fast for Imogene to follow.

"I didn't know you would be back so soon, or I would've waited for you. I could think of no other way to stop Henry. The butler didn't believe me."

The inventor let out a tiny sigh and seemed to be trying to force herself to relax. "What happened?"

Imogene looked at her hands. Unable to speak. So embarrassed and humiliated and ashamed and hurt. But she must say something. Her hips were bad, bone bruised by the queen's grip. She wouldn't be able to work today.

Genevieve's hand covered her clasped ones. Comfort again. She really wasn't angry with her.

"She also didn't believe me."

"And?"

"She tried to…" Imogene couldn't say it out loud.

The hand left hers and came up to the collar of her best dress. A dress now likely ruined for having been slept in. Besides which, Imogene couldn't stand the memory of what had happened while she wore it. Or what had almost happened.

"May I? Please?"

Imogene was powerless against the begging in Genevieve's voice. "I should love to be out of this dress," she admitted.

The inventor released the top few buttons and with shaking fingers explored Imogene's neck under the heavy fall of her hair. She let out a long sigh.

Imogene forced herself to go on. "Not that. She didn't try that." She waved a hand down at her aching hips. "She wanted… you know."

"Oh, you poor thing." Genevieve instantly stopped touching her. "How could she? And you innocent of all that. Disgusting! Imogene, I am so very sorry."

Imogene tried to lighten the mood. "She didn't get very far. I threatened her with your friend, Lady Maccon."

Genevieve let out a bark of surprised laughter.

"She let me go. Nothing really happened. I'm a little frightened, and rather bruised, but not sullied in any way." She didn't want to lose all vestige of respect in Genevieve's eyes.

"But to torture you with something so alien to your nature."

Imogene wanted to protest that was not the problem at all, it was simply that she was not interested in the *countess* that way. Surely, the inventor wouldn't toss her on the bed and hold her down? Then again, Imogene likely outweighed Genevieve; if anyone was going to be tossed...

"So, what would make you feel better? Tea? Toast? A bath?" The inventor turned practical.

"A bath sounds heavenly, but you don't have to fuss."

"Of course I have to fuss, *choupinette*. And I will contact Alexia immediately."

Genevieve went and yanked on the bell rope.

The new daytime parlourmaid appeared.

"Have a bath sent up immediately."

The maid bobbed a curtsy and vanished.

"Why contact Lady Maccon?" Imogene wondered, trying to figure out how to move without aches.

"Why, to arrange your relocation, of course. You cannot possibly wish to stay. Alexia runs an excellent household. I am sure she can find something for a girl of your skills. Biffy, at the very least, could put you to work in the hat shop – with your head for mathematics you would be running the place inside a week."

"But I don't want to move to London and work in a *hat shop!*" *I want to stay here, with you.* "No one will trouble me now that you're home. Henry can't…"

"Henry will be sacked, and possibly castrated if I have my way. But even I cannot entirely control the countess. If she has serious designs on you, I am not confident in my ability to protect you."

"Don't those cravat-pin darts of yours work on vampires?"

Genevieve laughed. "Well, yes, and you should begin wearing one immediately. But to be truly safe, I must remove you from the hive entirely."

"I don't want to leave. I knew the dangers when I first came to work here." *At one time I embraced the dangers, because I wanted any attention in that arena. Although I didn't know the queen's perversions were also violent.* The drones always seemed so happy to be summoned to her chambers. *Perhaps she is only violent with me because I have defied her.*

A knock on the door heralded two footmen with the bathtub.

"Which one of you is Henry?" Genevieve demanded, standing up from the bed and marching over to the tall young men.

The chambermaids came in with pitchers of hot

water and began to fill the tub. Suddenly, there were a great many people in the room.

Henry stepped forward and bowed, looking cocky and not scared at all. Although Imogene had never before heard such a cold tone in her dear inventor's voice.

Madame Lefoux stepped in towards him, reached down to the crotch of his britches, grabbed, squeezed, and then twisted. Henry howled in surprised misery.

The second footman took a step forward.

Genevieve looked at him. "Don't you *dare* interfere."

He stepped back again quickly.

"Like to prey on women, do you? Like to bruise in places that won't be noticed? Like to lord your miniscule bit of power over those weaker than yourself?" Madame Lefoux's teeth were clenched and she squeezed all the tighter. Henry was clawing at her wrists in a desperate attempt to get her to let go.

She did so and Henry crumpled.

The inventor crouched over him. Some sort of avenging pixie dressed as a dandy. "I am not a violent woman, as a rule. It is uncivilized. However, in your case, I make an exception." She then crashed the palm of her hand into Henry's eye.

"Stop, please," said Imogene. One might have thought she would enjoy revenge. Seeing her nemesis brought low. But she didn't wish to see Genevieve do it. Didn't like seeing her idol descend to Henry's level.

"Quite right, my dear." The inventor stood, looming over the cowering footman. "You are dismissed. I shall inform the hive that they must search anew for a matched set of footmen. You may tell whomever you are *really* working for that those notes you stole are intentionally flawed. I knew, you see, all along. You will get nowhere with them. Now get up, and get out."

Henry got.

"You" – Madame Lefoux pointed at the second footman – "tell the butler that Henry has been discharged for spying on my experiments and stealing my research. He should be escorted off the grounds and given neither reference nor character."

The bath full, Henry gone, and the other servants fled, Imogene hauled herself slowly out of bed.

She couldn't raise her arms and with hips aching, she had to shuffle instead of walk. She didn't know quite how to manage it, but she *would* bathe!

"I had best step out. Should I call one of the maids to help you?" Genevieve's voice had lost its authority and was oddly hesitant.

Imogene was horrified by the idea of one of her former colleagues being obliged to tend to her bruises. "I know it's a terrible imposition, but would you mind? I feel safer with you."

The inventor let out a shaky breath. "Of course."

Then Genevieve began to unbutton Imogene's gown.

In Imogene's fantasies, such a thing had often occurred but never under such circumstances. Genevieve was as solicitous as any nurse, stripping her out of the dress with infinite care.

"Give it away, please?" Imogene would have liked to burn it, but she couldn't accept such waste.

Madame Lefoux tossed it aside. She took a breath as though fortifying herself for some unpleasant task.

Am I repulsive now? "I think I can manage," said Imogene at that, "if you'd rather not."

"Hush, *choupinette*, do not be silly."

Genevieve unlaced her stays, and came back around to kneel, and pop open the busk of Imogene's corset, leaving her standing in nothing but thin chemise and stockings.

Thank heavens, I had the wherewithal to remove my boots before I got into bed last night.

Genevieve rolled down the stockings and Imogene stepped free. The inventor was looking strangely ill – a sheen of perspiration on her brow, teeth sunk into her lower lip.

Then she led Imogene to the tub. There she eased the chemise over Imogene's head and turn away, busying herself with laying it on the vanity. Imogene took that to mean she should climb into the tub.

It was a laborious process, her hips screamed at her, and it took much longer than she liked.

The inventor must have turned back too soon, because she heard a sharp hiss of indrawn breath. No doubt the queen's finger marks were clearly visible, a set of dark bruises on Imogene's white hips. And on her arms as well.

She sank into the water.

Behind her, Genevieve let out a sigh of relief. Then she began bustling about.

"Now, what else can I get you? I've found one of your work dresses and a clean chemise. I think with those bruises, you should forgo the corset. I do not know why you bother, really, you have a splendid figure without the darned thing. Oh, I *am* sorry, I am nattering. I forgot myself. No insult intended, Miss Hale."

Imogene's thoughts bounded between the fact that Genevieve admired her figure and the fact that she was now once again *Miss Hale*.

"That's all right. You're right. No stays. My stockings are in the basket next to my cot, and there should be clean drawers there as well."

The inventor continued to fuss.

Imogene relaxed into the warm water. Soaking away both Henry's touch and that of Countess Nadasdy.

Genevieve eventually worked up the courage to approach and hand Imogene a bar of vanilla-scented soap (which explained a great deal). Imogene scrubbed what she could with her limited range of motion. The soap was milk soft and finer than anything she'd ever used. *From Paris, perhaps?*

Genevieve left the chamber for a quarter of an hour, returning with a tray loaded with tea, fresh bread, two apples, and a wedge of hard cheese.

Imogene realized that she was starving and the water was beginning to cool. Her hair felt sticky. She didn't want to ask, but she couldn't see to it herself, and she so rarely got the luxury of a full bath.

"I wonder if I could trouble you to wash my hair?"

The inventor shook her head in an unsettled way but said, "Of course," and came reluctantly over.

Imogene suppressed an odd desire to cry as she bowed her head under Genevieve's ministrations. The inventor rubbed the soap-bar through Imogene's thick dark hair and then worked it to a lather with her fingertips. It was a wonderful feeling. She really had the gentlest hands.

Although Imogene did wince at one point, when a wayward lock escaped and slapped against the side of her damaged face.

"Oh, Imogene. Why on earth didn't you tell me about the footman earlier?"

"Men have picked on me all my life. You don't go around looking like me and rejecting them without punishment."

"Always rejecting them, then?"

"I don't want *them*!" Imogene couldn't keep the frustration out of her voice. It was the frustration causing her to cry more than anything else. That Genevieve could be so kind and yet still so far away.

"Poor little *choupinette*," said the object of her frustration. "You have been through too much. Let me get these suds out and put you to bed."

Imogene closed her eyes under a pitcher of clean water and then allowed herself to be pulled to standing and helped out of the tub, the inventor supporting a great deal of her weight – she was stronger than she looked.

Briskly, as if she were a small child, Genevieve wrapped her in a thick, fuzzy towel and rubbed her dry. There were no more comments on her injuries, and she seemed neither repulsed nor attracted by Imogene's bruised body.

It was too much, so Imogene let the tears trickle down her face.

A large silk handkerchief was pressed to her nose. "Blow."

Imogene blew.

"Now, back to bed you go. No, my bed, it is easier."

Imogene didn't protest.

Genevieve tucked her in, tender hands spreading her hair out over the pillow to dry. Then she handed her a cup of tea, at which juncture Imogene stopped crying.

Genevieve settled softly on the edge of the bed and fed her bread and cheese. Imogene ate most of it, then fell into a deep, vanilla-scented sleep.

Henry was long gone by the time she woke. The butler had been reprimanded for not listening to Imogene. There was a militant expression in Genevieve's green eyes that suggested, once the sun set, the vampire queen was next to be scolded.

Imogene wasn't sure who would come out on top with those two.

There was a small, warm weight next to her hip, and at her movement, two bright black eyes and a set of ridiculously fluffy ears perked up. Someone had let Skoot in. She put a hand down to caress those silly ears and he wriggled in pleasure.

The inventor hadn't gone to the potting shed,

much to Imogene's surprise, but was sitting at a little escritoire near a window, wearing a set of spectacles and sorting through a stack of correspondence.

Imogene lay, petting Skoot, and watched her for a while. She allowed herself to admire the elegant curve of the other woman's neck as she bent to read. There it was again – peeking out the back, exposed by her short hair – some kind of scar?

"Is that a birthmark?" Imogene's voice was husky with too much sleep. As the inventor had now seen all of Imogene, it seemed a less intrusive question.

Genevieve looked up and smiled – dimples flashed. She rose and came to Imogene's side.

"You are awake. How do you feel?"

"Much improved, thank you. Less sore because of the bath, and in better spirits. I'm sorry I was so sentimental earlier. I didn't mean to cry."

"Perfectly understandable, do not even think upon it. You look better too."

"What time is it?"

"Gone three."

"I'm glad I woke then. Sleep any more and I should never rest tonight."

"Are you hungry?"

"In a bit. Would you sit next to me a moment first?" Imogene was not above using her invalid status to garner more contact and attention.

Genevieve removed Skoot, mock-reprimanding him in French, and folded herself into his spot next to Imogene. Much to Imogene's delight, the inventor took hold of her hand in a reassuring clasp. There was nothing sexual about it, yet it felt nice.

"What is the mark on your neck?" Imogene asked again. "At first I thought you'd been bitten, but it's too dark, almost black, and not shaped right."

The inventor actually blushed. "It is a tattoo of an octopus. I belong to a sort of club and it has become rather a totem animal of mine."

"Not the wicker chicken?"

"No, that is someone else's totem. It was an octopus that landed me here."

"It was?" Imogene was all ears.

"I built a massive octomaton and went rather wild with it. Knocked down the old hive house in London. And a few other houses, too. The countess had kidnapped my boy, you see? I had no other choice. Well, I maybe did have other choices, but I didn't think so at the time."

Imogene could understand. If Genevieve was so fiercely protective of a mere assistant, she must be awesome in defense of someone she truly loved.

"What happened?"

"Alexia. That is, Lady Maccon. She worked a deal whereby Quesnel would be kept by the hive. It has to do with the legal standing of his blood mother – he is not my child by birth, you see, but by adoption – anyway… Where was I? Oh, yes. Quesnel would stay with the hive here until he reached his majority at eighteen. I would be indentured for ten years, in order to stay with him, and as punishment for the octopus terrorizing London incident. Then, of course, Quesnel had his own opinion on the matter and convinced us both – the countess and I – that he would be best going away to university early." She paused then. "He was right. He's thriving at L'École des Arts et Métiers." Pride suffused her voice.

"But it left you here alone, without him."

"Not so bad." The dimples were back. "I have you now."

I'm not your daughter, Imogene wanted to say. But instead, she basked in the glow of those dimples. *She does like me,* Imogene decided. *It's just she's holding herself back. And it has to do with some other part of her past.* She took solace in the fact that this had been a breakthrough of sorts, learning what had caused Genevieve's indenture. Imogene would be patient and learn more. Learn enough to chip away at the inventor's reticence.

CHAPTER EIGHT

In Which There Are More Dimples

The queen made no further moves in Imogene's direction. Unfortunately, neither did Genevieve.

For a full two months, Imogene resumed the established daily pattern – potting shed, sums, dimples, tea, lab, dimples, luncheon, equations, more dimples, supper, and if she was lucky, one last set of dimples before bed. The intimacy of that bath was never discussed, although the inventor seemed to have elected to throw herself into a caring parental role as a result.

What Genevieve failed to realize was that Imogene was just as stubborn as she, only quieter about it. *All I have is my beauty. Surely it won't fail me the one time I really wish to apply it?*

Imogene was determined to try her hand at seduction. Remembering the way the village girls pursued their flirts, she set out to wage a similar war. Of course, she knew full well she was nowhere near good enough for the inventor, but surely they could at least share a bed? Imogene wouldn't ask for anything more. (Although what *more* was there between two women? Certainly not marriage. Not in England, anyway.)

In the laboratory, Imogene concocted reasons to touch her inventor. A hand to her arm, a press against her side when they were both crouched to examine something. Some device would spark and Imogene would gasp, reaching for Genevieve's hand.

The inventor would blush, or nudge back, then seem to remember herself and pull away. She clearly wanted more, but she didn't respond in a manner that encouraged Imogene to press further.

Once, leaning over Imogene to consult on a sum, Genevieve forgot her reserve. A hand, cool and rough-skinned, caressed the back of Imogene's neck, fingers dipping into her hair. Imogene leaned into the touch, turning her head to inhale vanilla, pressing her cheek into the other woman's bare wrist (her sleeves were rolled up as usual). Imogene dared to brush her lips on the delicate white skin there.

Genevieve let out a little whimper. The needy murmur was so quiet, yet it cut through the clattering of machinery to sting Imogene's ears. Her inventor sounded both frustrated and very sad.

Imogene stopped the kiss and pulled back. Crushed. *I don't want to hurt her. Lord, that's the opposite of what I want. How do I beat this? How do I fight for what I want when the object of my desire is holding everything away from me despite herself?* Imogene wished she had someone, anyone she could ask for help. Any words she might say or actions she might take that would encourage Genevieve to open to her. If only a little. But she didn't know what she was battling against. *This is the emotional equivalent of a fistfight with an octopus.*

Still Imogene persisted, trying to prove that her interest was genuine. She found herself in a heightened state of awareness most days, attuned to the inventor's smell, the way her hips moved under her trousers, the tendons in her hands, the sound of her voice. She ached to press tiny kisses to the corners of her mouth. She wished to know how the rest of Genevieve's skin tasted. She wanted whimpers, just not sad ones.

Imogene was also painfully aware of her own experience with Henry. She refused to impose herself as he had done. She took pains to be more tempting than predatory. Making a great effort with her appearance, fixing her hair high and soft to show her neck. Pinching color into her cheeks.

She caught Genevieve looking a great deal. Looking but never again touching, or even talking much beyond pleasantries and instructions. Those green eyes stayed hungry, and they stayed sad.

And while Imogene lay restless and aching in her own cot, she swore she could hear, in the other room, Genevieve tossing and turning just as much.

They might have gone on forever this way (although Imogene suspected she would have burned to a crisp with her own wanting were that the case) except that the countess tried again.

Imogene had become almost comfortable with her routine and she was careful to be in their bedchamber by nightfall (well, Genevieve's bedchamber), but with the autumn full upon them and the nights getting longer, they didn't always manage to finish in the potting shed before dark.

Imogene had intended to nip out and check on an experiment while Madame Lefoux took a bath. Unfortunately, the experiment ran longer than expected, and by the time it finished, the sun had set.

She hurried up the servants' stairs, avoiding everyone she could. The staff were all mostly frightened of her since Madame Lefoux's display of defensive squeezing. (Witnessed by some, it was thus known by all.)

Unfortunately, Imogene couldn't stick entirely to the servants' section; there was always the part where she must walk down the main hallway to get to the bedroom door.

She hurried along, head down, hand to her cravat pin.

Countess Nadasdy flitted before her. Vampires walked so silently, it was impossible to hear them coming. The hive queen was wearing a dinner gown of ruched cream lace with an over-jacket of blue brocade. It was very beautiful and very expensive. It also looked, to Imogene's untrained eye, ever so slightly like an undergarment.

Imogene brandished her cravat pin.

"No need for that, my dear child."

"Oh, I think there might be."

"What are you doing to my inventor?"

"Me?"

"She has been overly flustered of late. As much as you are protected by Lady Maccon's patronage, so Madame Lefoux is protected by mine. Whether she likes it or not. And I've noticed her to be quite... off lately. Why is that, do you think?"

"I've no idea," lied Imogene.

"I'm sure you don't. Are you two having... difficulties?" The vampire grimaced as if to imply that the affairs of mortals were so trivial, it pained her to enquire. Then she added, "Do you need someone to explain the necessary details? A demonstration, perhaps?"

Well, yes. But not you! Imogene backed away, edging towards Genevieve's bedroom door.

"Kind of you to offer, but I'm sure we don't need your help, ma'am."

The queen didn't look convinced. She followed, stalking.

Imogene found her back against the door. One hand still clutching the cravat pin, she turned the knob with the other. *Safety!*

"Mortals. Everything is so complicated with you." Countess Nadasdy looked even more disgusted.

Imogene closed the door in her face and leaned back against it, letting out a shaky breath.

A dainty fist with supernatural power behind it hit the door from the other side.

Imogene jumped away, heart racing.

Madame Lefoux, who appeared to have fallen asleep in her bath before the fire, was out of it and across the room in a trice, dripping and gloriously naked.

"Are you all right, Imogene?"

"She is quite horrible!" Imogene attempted to thread the cravat pin back into her dress collar with shaky hands.

Genevieve tutted, took the pin, and did it for her. Imogene could hardly breathe, to have a wet, naked Genevieve so close to her.

Then, sensing that Imogene was reacting to her proximity, the inventor grabbed a towel and wrapped it around herself.

Imogene banged her own head, much less violently, back against the door. "This is ridiculous!"

"Did she try with you again?"

"She suggested we might need her help in figuring things out. You and I, between us." The statement hung in the air like a damp sponge, dripping with implications.

Madame Lefoux closed her eyes in horror. "I am *so sorry*. I never meant my preferences to impact you. She misconstrues your inclinations because I made you my assistant. That she would even suggest such a thing must offend and shock."

Imogene marched over and stood with her hands on her hips. She fixed Genevieve's green eyes with her own brown ones.

"For goodness' sake! She certainly does *not* misconstrue my inclinations. The only insult extended is that I might choose her over you! I am not interested in men. I have never been with a man and do not ever intend to be so. For as long as I can recall, I have only ever looked at girls. This is not something you have done to me, nor some insult she has foisted upon me. *This is the way I am.*"

Breathless, Imogene leaned in. Frankly, she felt some small sympathy for the vampires and their needs after so many months of denial. She pressed her lips to those of the inventor, who was standing, stunned, and still only in a towel.

This was absolutely fine by Imogene.

When Genevieve didn't respond to the impassioned embrace, Imogene's heart sank.

She backed off and hung her head. Her gaze focused on Genevieve's long legs – still dripping. "Since that first walk in the garden, you are all I have thought of. I'm at a loss. How to convince you? I'm not half good enough, I know, no more than a parlourmaid, and trouble for you with the hive. But I'm also not her. Whoever she was who hurt you so. I'm not! I deserve a chance. I shouldn't be blamed for the sins of some other woman. Unless it is that truly you do not want me. If you don't think we'd suit... if you don't want... then perhaps we should reconsider the terms of my indenture. I don't wish to be an imposition. I—"

The inventor kissed her.

It became patently obvious that she did indeed have a great deal more experience than Imogene. But Imogene was a good student, tilting her head, relaxing her mouth, allowing Genevieve's tongue to sweep through.

God, her lips were so soft, and she tasted of vanilla too. Sweet, or maybe that was Imogene's imagination, her nose playing tricks on her palate. Imogene felt her brain seize up, like an engine without oil. All she could feel was that tongue, a wet brand, and those lips, and the inventor's vanilla scent tendrilled about her.

When Genevieve would have pulled away, Imogene refused to allow it. Desperately she chased her lips, offering hers up again. Her hands were frantic and a great deal more bold than if she'd been thinking about what she was doing. She wanted to touch every piece of skin not covered by the towel. Oh, very well, she wanted to touch under the towel too.

Genevieve caught the frenzy driving Imogene and molded it. Returning touch for touch, kiss for kiss in a restrained fury. Her cool, callused hands, damp from the bath, seemed just as frantically interested in mapping Imogene's body. Stroking over the fabric of her dress, testing the weight of the flesh beneath.

If Imogene had imagined anything, it had been moving slowly. She'd fantasized about stripping Genevieve of her layers, one masculine piece at a time to show the female body underneath, lean and muscled and sweetly curved.

But Genevieve was already stripped and Imogene wished for nothing more than to be bare herself. To press her body fully against Genevieve's. But she couldn't unbutton her own dress without stepping away, and if she stepped away, the inventor might come to her senses. Might decide to stop everything so as to save Imogene from exploitation.

Then, blessedly, Genevieve's fingers were fumbling with those very buttons, working one after another, trembling slightly. The high collar was smoothed back so the inventor might lay reverent little kisses about Imogene's neck and down to the swell of her breasts above her chemise. Imogene had stopped wearing stays. If Genevieve thought she looked better without her corset, then she would never wear a corset again.

And then, horrible stillness.

Imogene wasn't certain what happened; perhaps the inventor's hand brushed against the cravat pin. A reminder of what had nearly occurred in the hall. Imogene's own hands stilled in reaction, tingling with the memory of smooth, damp skin.

Genevieve backed away with an expression of horror on her face. Then she whirled and fled the room.

Imogene wanted to cry.

But she was also determined. Genevieve must come back eventually (it was, after all, *her* room), and Imogene would be ready. With quick hands she stripped and, pulling pins from her hair, let it down. Genevieve liked her hair; occasionally, when she wasn't being overly cautious, Imogene had caught her touching a loose strand.

Moments later, the inventor returned.

"I'm only wearing a towel! *Merde*." She closed the door with a bang and turned to find Imogene, now utterly naked, standing before the fire.

Imogene firmed her lips, narrowed her eyes, and glared.

Genevieve Lefoux, famous inventor, generally charming, usually forceful, looked utterly terrified.

Imogene stalked towards her.

"This is not a good idea, *choupinette*. I am far too old for you."

"Good, you've some experience in these matters. So, come to bed with me, Genevieve."

"I will corrupt you."

"Exactly what I'm hoping for." Imogene took her firmly by the hand and began to lead her to the big bed.

"You are too much, Imogene. You are too exactly what I have always wanted. You are too beautiful, and too good-natured, and too loyal. I cannot trust you."

Imogene winced at that. "Only one night, Genevieve. I'm not asking you to trust me with anything more." Although of course she wanted that terribly.

She released the inventor's hand and lay back. Offering herself, because the only possible way forward was for Genevieve to choose in truth.

Choose me, please. I will do the best I can, I promise. "I'm a quick study, Genevieve, you know I am. Just tonight, come to bed."

The inventor gave a sigh of acceptance, and relief, and possibly joy, dropped the towel, and came to bed.

Genevieve Lefoux had dimples when she smiled. She also had two little divots above the swell of her bottom that Imogene decided were also dimples.

Imogene got to lick all the dimples.

Beneath her tongue, Genevieve writhed and

murmured praise or curses – difficult to know as she spoke her native language. Imogene wished she could understand French. But she was learning without instruction either way. She memorized the taste and texture of the other woman's skin – where it thinned over the points of hip and elbow, where it plumped over muscles in arms and legs, where it softened into stomach and thighs. She nuzzled into the belly button, the long indentation of spine, the backs of knees.

Genevieve's responses were glorious. Little whimpers, the occasional twitch from a ticklish spot, and when Imogene chose well, a moan. Imogene paid careful attention to those moans, returning for more, to the muscles on Genevieve's upper back, the sides of her neck, the nipples on her small breasts. Nibbles, much to her delight, got louder moans (and even some wiggling).

Genevieve grabbed her up and kissed her; out of frustration or a need to participate more, it mattered not. It was a wonderful thing to kiss back, Imogene's tongue pressing into a sweet vanilla mouth as she draped her naked curved weight over her inventor's leaner frame. She didn't know skin could tingle so. She didn't know the rush of color behind closed eyes as Genevieve traced a path over her body with firm hands. Hands that were both sure and curious, dipping and stroking and squeezing. Hands that also trembled, with fear or nerves. Imogene could do nothing to allay that fear but offer more of herself. Offer up everything on a wish to be trusted.

She'd no idea that the awful ache she'd been feeling for months could intensify into something so completely unbearable and then crash over into a pleasure so intense and sweet, she was left shaking.

She also didn't realize what an utter joy it could be to bring such pleasure to another person. Not once but several times.

"What do you know," she said, looking up from between the inventor's legs with a cheeky grin. "I've found the x."

Genevieve laughed. "You're sure you've not done this before?" Then she gasped.

Imogene had her mouth full and elected not to answer.

"I suppose… you do not use that tongue of yours very often… you must have been… saving it… for something." Genevieve's voice was hoarse and stuttering.

Imogene flicked her tongue over the x.

Genevieve switched back to French for a while. Finally, in frustration, she cried, "Why… do you not speak my language? It is so much more suited… to this… Oh!"

In answer, Imogene twirled her tongue and pressed, and Genevieve splintered under her ministrations, losing all her words, even the French ones.

Then Genevieve shifted her over and went on her own equation-solving quest. Less tentative, more driven. Imogene blushed to think on the noises she herself made as a result.

Eventually, they were too exhausted to continue.

Imogene's heart was willing but her body was wrung out.

She rose to take to her own bed. She understood their agreement. One night was all Genevieve had promised, and the dawn was coming.

The inventor's sleepy voice, rich with a full coloring of French silkiness, said, "Please stay."

Imogene had noticed that in times of great stress, or excitement, or (apparently) pleasure, Genevieve's accent became more pronounced.

So she stayed, and curled against her inventor, feeling sweat-soaked and satisfied.

Perhaps if she were very, very good, they might do it again someday.

"That can never happen again, Miss Hale."

Imogene woke to the voice of her inventor, roughened by sleep, and callused fingers stroking through the long tangle of her hair.

They were curled together, legs entwined, but Genevieve had already left the bed, for all her body still resided there. No doubt the inventor had thought it all through and decided that in order to protect Imogene, and protect herself, last night had been a horrible mistake.

Imogene sighed and rolled away into a bright beam of sunlight. It didn't have to be so cheery, did it? *I'm back to Miss Hale. How came my own name to sound so sad?*

She slumped into the mattress in frustration and stared up at the ceiling. "I know, only one night. But it was wonderful, wasn't it?"

She was pretty darn certain, now, that the attraction was mutual.

"It was glorious," replied the inventor. She was always one to give credit were it was due.

"There, see. I'm good for something beyond equations."

"Miss Hale, I will not take advantage of you like this."

"I think you might call me Imogene, at this juncture." Her voice was more sarcastic than she liked. She tried to pull herself back to dourness and reserve. To that place where she kept her secret close, nose up-tilted, and sleepwalked through her own existence.

"It is not right."

"And I shall call you Genevieve."

"You are too young."

"No, I'm not. Stop looking for excuses."

"You deserve some nice young woman who will give you all her heart, and not some old broken tom with too much history and no ability to love again. I've been sucked dry, *choupinette*. There's nothing left here but some superficial flirting."

Imogene would not believe that. "Nonsense, you love your work. You love your son. You even love Lady Maccon, in a strange way."

"That is not the same thing."

"There must be something left for me. I would settle for very little." *For now, but I want all of it. Heart. Body. Skin against skin. Long nights and lazy mornings.* But she could never say that. Genevieve would find it terrifying.

The inventor sat up and turned away to sit on the edge of the mattress. Her shoulders were hunched in regret. Imogene rolled to her side and placed a tentative hand on the small of the other woman's back.

"Tell me why, at least?" Imogene didn't add that she was owed that courtesy; she wasn't sure she was. After all, she'd pushed and pushed, knowing the other woman must have good reason for her reluctance.

"Has no one spoken to you of Quesnel's mother? His blood mother, I mean. Gossip in the servants' hall?"

"No. But I haven't asked. It seemed wrong, too painful a subject."

"Angelique." Genevieve's voice was tinged with tones Imogene had never heard before – flat and blurred. It was like she'd lost all the French off her tongue.

"She was very beautiful. Like you. Only all sunlight where you are the moon. She had the biggest eyes you ever saw, pansy violet they were. Quesnel has her eyes. And her hair, all silken blonde. She was French like me, changeable and quick. Had some training as a spy, although not many knew that. We met young, parted ways, then met again when we were old enough to know ourselves better. She was pregnant by then. I adored her. I would have walked through a boiler barefoot for her. She had Quesnel soon after and we were as much a family as women like me…" She paused and tilted her face to one side, glancing at Imogene out of the corner of her eye.

"Women like *us* ever get."

Imogene let out a long breath. Well, that was some victory in acceptance at last. "What happened?"

The inventor turned to face her but wasn't seeing her at all. Her green eyes were focused on some memory of pain, as if by watching it again the hurt could be dulled. Only, it seemed to sharpen and cut anew.

Imogene realized that Genevieve reminded herself of this often. It was a tool she used to slice herself, with guilt or shame, so that she remembered to withdraw from the world. This was a wound she reopened constantly so it never scabbed over, and never healed. She was bleeding ghosts instead of blood. And she did it out of some morbid need to punish herself.

Imogene's heart sank. She was strong enough to fight for the possibility of *now*, but a *now* could never be won, fencing with ghosts.

Genevieve continued, "It was not enough. I was not good enough, or strong enough. Family wasn't enough. We weren't enough."

Imogene shook her head, confused. How could anyone want more than Genevieve? What more was there to want? Except…

"Immortality?"

The inventor nodded. "She left me for a hive and its queen. And service to both. She was a very fine lady's maid. And a decent spy. She could not take Quesnel with her, you see? Drones are not supposed to have children. Although they found out eventually and tried to take him anyway."

Her face was so drawn, Imogene thought with horror, that the dimples might never return.

"I could not follow her. I'm not good at sharing. And even if I wanted immortality, which I don't, what good would it do us? The odds against either of us surviving are astronomically small, let alone both. And then what? An eternal life apart. Vampire queens cannot share a territory, let alone a house. So, I let her go, because she wanted it more than she wanted me. To love someone is to allow them their dreams, no? Even if you do not share those dreams. And I tried to protect her, *mon dieu*, I tried. And I tried to protect our son."

"What happened?" Imogene was almost too scared to ask.

"She died. Not trying for metamorphosis. Just some stupid fall, on some stupid assignment in Scotland. *And* she went to ghost."

"Oh, God." Imogene blinked. She was crying. Not for this girl she'd never known – how *dare* anyone break Genevieve's heart – but for the soul-deep hurt in her lover's eyes. "So, she might have made queen?"

Genevieve nodded. "She might."

"I don't want immortality."

"Oh, Imogene, it is not that. It is not her. It is me. There are some who drift through life with so much love. They give readily and easily. I think, perhaps, Lady Maccon is one of these. And her husband. And my son. It is a heady thing for them – they are constantly replenished, like a fountain. So, they may give again, and do so generously. And there are some of us who have only a finite amount, like a puddle. I doled out all of mine already. It is stepped in and muddied, splashed away and gone."

Imogene nodded, understanding. Not accepting, but understanding. "No drops left for me?"

"You deserve so much more than drops. You should have a lake spread out before you. You should be the first thing I think of in the morning and the last thing at night. But you are not. I think of her. And I always will."

Imogene gave a watery smile. "I suspect that sometimes, you may be thinking of inventions. I've seen you get up in the small hours, scribbling notes."

"You do not need to be kind about this."

Imogene had her pride. It wasn't a noble's pride but it was there, keeping her from begging. "You warned me. I came into this with my eyes open. Well, not totally, but enough." She came over mulish, and moved her hand up the other woman's back to the tattoo at the top. *A slight raising of skin, another mark. Another sign of something else Genevieve once loved.* Imogene stroked the divot of her inventor's spine back down to the place where those two dimples rested.

"We could still gertrude."

"What?"

"Well, I figured the opposite of rodgering is gertruding."

The inventor let out a puff of surprised laughter. "You are remarkable, you know that?"

"No, I'm a perverted parlourmaid whom you have elevated beyond her station. And I shall try to do my best to earn it, regardless of how we proceed from here."

"It would be too easy to love you."

"But not for you?"

"But not for me."

Imogene's heart sank. *Rotten luck for me. Genevieve Lefoux is also too easy to love.*

Imogene did try to stay optimistic, but she wasn't particularly optimistic by nature. No one would ever call her cheerful. Even-tempered as a compliment, grave as a question, and arrogant as an insult. Heartbroken, Imogene fell into all three with a vengeance.

She focused hard on her work. Genevieve did the same. And while Imogene still loved her job, she was, frankly, miserable. She moped. She hungered. She craved. It was all very melodramatic, which only made her frustrated with herself.

Their conversation was not so relaxed as it had once been, their moving together around the potting shed not so easy. The clattering, huffing noises of the laboratory, which Imogene had once found comforting, grated on her nerves.

The aching tension of need returned.

In fact, for Imogene, the wanting was worse than before. Now she knew *exactly* what she was missing. Late at night, she touched herself instead, but it was nowhere near as good. It didn't seem to have much of an effect on the need, either. The more they were in each other's company, the more she battled her desire to kiss and to caress, not for possession but for connection.

Imogene stopped flirting. It tortured her just as much as it did Genevieve. She still caught the inventor watching her, longing in her gaze. Imogene stopped reaching out, despite the ache. She knew Genevieve did the same. Many times the inventor's hand twitched in her direction and then fell back against a trouser leg, unsatisfied.

It wasn't fair. To tell her no and then to still look so.

Of course, it occurred to Imogene to hope that perhaps the inventor was fooling herself. Time had passed. Perhaps she could love again. But she was so very stubborn, and the hurt in her voice had been so fresh. Imogene was forced to constantly remind herself – no fencing with ghosts. The human with the sword always ended up looking ridiculous.

The only thing that noticeably changed was that they now used each other's first names. Their midday meals were awkward things, scrabbling to find a topic that didn't touch on delicate territory.

At one such luncheon, Imogene asked something she'd wondered for a while. "Why the potting shed?"

Genevieve looked about, startled. "Oh, I suppose it is a little odd. Frankly, it is a traditional place of science. Used to accommodate a professor friend of mine, when the werewolves were here. I had it expanded, of course. He used it for sheep pickling."

"Training sheep in how to pickle?" Imogene asked, confused.

"No, for pickling the sheep themselves."

Imogene choked and then coughed in surprise.

"Werewolf thing. I would not think on it too closely." Genevieve picked at her food.

She's not eating very well these days. Imogene worried, and subtly tried to push the cheese in her direction. Didn't the French love cheese?

The inventor appeared not to see it.

CHAPTER NINE

In Which Werewolves Meddle

"*She* wants a word with us," said Genevieve, coming back from her customary supper with the hive.

Imogene was sitting at the escritoire, reading a book of poetry. Skoot was curled on her feet. She hadn't registered the time or she would've sent him down. The vampires always looked for him after supper.

Genevieve whistled him out and closed the door.

Imogene had grown to like poetry, now that she understood more of the words. She couldn't handle the heady stuff, like Wordsworth. But then Genevieve pooh-poohed Wordsworth out of hand as overly British. Instead, she'd found Imogene a slim volume of someone called Sappho in translation. In fact, she'd made it a gift.

Imogene was incandescent about it. She'd never before possessed a real live book of her own. Occasionally, when she could work up the courage, they'd discuss one of the poems, long into the evening. Both of them talking a great deal, so that they didn't touch, yearning, until it became unbearable and Imogene would flee to her cot, to yearn alone.

"Countess Nadasdy?" she asked, as if there could be any other *she* Genevieve would refer to in *that* tone of voice.

"Yes. And she is unhappy about something."

"Isn't she always?"

"Good point."

"I don't see what she has to complain about. You've had two papers accepted by the Royal Society, and that little throwaway poggle-whizzer gadget is selling extremely well."

"*We* have had two papers." Genevieve insisted on sharing a byline with Imogene these days, although Imogene protested she was only the assistant. All she did was the sums and maybe a little tinkering with a wrench.

"Still, she wants us, even specified you should come with me. You'll be all right?"

Imogene nodded. "She doesn't scare me like she used to. If anything, I feel a little sorry for her." Unsaid was the fact that, now she knew what it was like to couple with a woman, Imogene could see what the vampire queen was after. She understood the thirst. And why a girl could come over tetchy when she was denied. *I could never believe any man as skilled with his tongue as Genevieve. Or I, for that matter.* Imogene praised herself shamelessly. *Although I could do with more practice.*

Countess Nadasdy was holding court in the

drawing room, all three of her hive mates with her.

"Good, you're here. Come forward."

Imogene and Genevieve went and stood before her, out of reach, for all the good that did them, given the general strength and speed of the four predators before them.

"Something of grave import has been brought to our attention. A report, in the Royal Society bulletin. A patent has been filed for a new sundowner bullet, from a Professor Swern. It is exactly the style and type you were working on, Genevieve. You remember, you showed me the prototype."

"Henry," breathed Imogene.

"No," said the countess, "You, I think."

Oh, here we go again.

"Don't be preposterous. What motive could Imogene possibly have?" Genevieve leapt to her defense.

"I need hardly tell you she has very little love for this hive, nor for vampires in general. Her behavior towards us indicates no affection or loyalty. I would suspect a great deal of money was laid on the table to buy her favor. I wanted the technology in order to keep it under control. Professor Swern has no indenture, so he will sell to the highest bidder. I understand the military is interested. I don't like it, don't like it at all. You, my dear little parlourmaid, have quite a motive."

"Why would I stay long enough for the theft to be noticed?" Imogene defended herself with logic.

Logic never worked on vampires. "Perhaps you thought you could lie to us and keep your place, steal more technology for revenge and profit. Perhaps there is something else holding you here." She glanced significantly at Genevieve.

The inventor blustered, "This is ridiculous. You are manufacturing the accusation to get rid of her."

The countess only sneered, showing a fang. "I have rendered judgment and the judgment of the hive is sacrosanct."

She gave a nod and two drones stepped forward, one to either side of Genevieve.

Imogene reached for her cravat pin.

Dr Caedes grabbed her. His mouth was open wide, his fangs clearly visible.

The countess gave a tight smile. "This is for your own good, Genevieve Lefoux. Can't you see this girl is killing you? You've lost a great deal of weight recently, and I suspect poison on top of everything else. You are my indenture, and your work is valuable to this hive. We cannot risk your health or her crafty ways. She is expendable. Doctor, if you would?"

The vampire ripped Imogene's gown, exposing one whole side of her neck. Imogene fought to keep herself from shaking. She fought to find her old faithful friend, that up-tilted nose. Arrogance in death. But she couldn't find it, because she didn't need it anymore; she had given it up for Genevieve.

Genevieve struggled futilely against the drones holding her. She arched up, kicking out and back, but they gripped vice-like and she couldn't break free.

The Duke of Hematol said, "This is a bad business, my queen. The girl is neither your indenture nor your drone."

"But it was *my* technology! It is my right to control my hive. Doctor, you may proceed."

A resounding crash at the front door, a rushing huffing noise, and suddenly the room was filled with dogs.

Not dogs, wolves.

Werewolves.

The biggest and the shaggiest of these stopped in front of Imogene, between her and the queen.

Lady Alexia Maccon, wearing a very nice plaid carriage dress, jumped off.

She'd been riding him.

Astride!

She raised what looked like an exceptionally ugly and rather frivolous parasol and pointed it at the vampire queen.

Her voice was calm and cool. "Now, now, now, Countess. That is *my* indenture. If you wish to have your house cleaned, I should be happy to do it for you." The parasol waved menacingly. Or it would have been menacing if it hadn't been so frilly.

Each vampire in the room was now flanked by two wolves. The largest one, whom Imogene had to assume was Lord Maccon, insinuated himself between her and Dr Caedes, breaking the vampire's grip almost casually.

One of the others, a big, beautiful white wolf with icy blue eyes, had separated Genevieve from her captors, knocking both drones down, and was standing over one with a look of wicked delight, growling.

Genevieve ran to Imogene and wrapped shaking

arms about her.

"I didn't think they would make it in time."

"You summoned the London Pack?"

"At supper, the moment the countess said she wished to see you tonight, I excused myself and sent an aetherogram to Lady Maccon."

Countess Nadasdy was on her feet. "You have no right to interfere! To invade my hive! Slavering dogs!"

Alexia Maccon made a *ppttttt* noise at the vampire queen. "I am *muhjah*." She gestured with her parasol at her wolf husband. "And he is *head of BUR*. I can guarantee that what you are doing to this girl violates both my authority and his. Which one of us would you prefer enacted justice?"

Lord Maccon bared his teeth and growled. It was a great deal scarier than when the white wolf did it.

Lord Ambrose leapt to protect his queen.

"It is my right to punish her. She stole hive secrets." Countess Nadasdy would not drop the false accusation. She was the doglike one at the moment, teeth sunk into an Imogene-shaped bone that she refused to let go.

Lady Maccon was not impressed. "Oh, yes? Have you proof?"

"She is poisoning Madame Lefoux!"

"Genevieve?"

"It is true, I have not been eating well, but that is…"

Lady Maccon finished the sentence for her. "More likely your fault than that poor girl's? Where is your proof, Countess?"

The queen only hissed. "But I *know* she did it. I want her gone!"

Lady Maccon sighed. "In the absence of proof, corporal punishment is not permitted, not even within a hive. However, I agree, I should remove Imogene from Woolsey for her own protection."

"No!" cried Genevieve, as if the word were wrested from her. "That is not what I wanted!"

Lady Maccon turned on her friend. "I'm beginning to think you don't know what you want, and poor Imogene is suffering for your indecision. Think of her well-being, my dear, do."

Genevieve fell silent.

The countess gave a truculent pout like a little child and not some centuries-old immortal. "Very well."

In an aside, Lady Maccon said to Imogene, "I should prefer we put this whole sorry mess to bed at this juncture. So, make your good-byes and we'll be off. Biffy, would you... Channing? You're volunteering? How bizarre." The big white wolf had trotted over and was waiting patiently at Imogene's side.

Genevieve, much to everyone's surprise (including, apparently, her own) kissed Imogene – swift and hard. Then, capturing her face in both callused hands, she said fiercely, "You'll love London."

Imogene nodded, mute and confused. *Except that you won't be there. And the laboratory won't be there. And Skoot, and—*

"Mount up," said Lady Maccon, not unkindly.

"You'll have to ride astride. Grab the ruff like so. Don't worry, pull as hard as you like, you can't hurt him. And in Channing's case, even if you could, he likely deserves it."

Imogene, much embarrassed, hiked up her skirts as Lady Maccon had demonstrated and slid astride the massive white wolf. She had to tuck up her legs, because she was taller than Lady Maccon, but Major Channing was as rangy a wolf as he was a man and carried her easily.

He lolled his tongue at her, delighted by her discomfort.

She wrapped her hands in his ruff.

"Got a good grip?" Lady Maccon asked.

Imogene nodded.

And they were off.

Imogene had never ridden a horse, so she'd no basis for comparison, but it was very fast. Werewolves could move with supernatural speed, and it seemed that in no time at all, they'd left Barking for the fields, then left the fields for the suburbs, then left the suburbs for the city.

London was amazing. It was bigger, and louder, and smokier than Imogene could've imagined. It was crowded with houses, cheek-to-cheek, and stacked on top of one another, filthy with soot. The streets were filled with all manner of humanity inside all manner of conveyance from carts to matched teams pulling elaborate carriages to steam locomotives to monowheels (she'd seen a sketch in the lab) and beyond.

Above the city, the sky seemed positively crowded with dirigibles. Imogene had thought the few she'd seen floating about the countryside were remarkable. These were even more impressive. Some were chubby postal carriers while other sleeker airships formed military floatillahs. There were tiny ones privately owned, and massive trans-Channel transports heading east.

The pack house was in (what Imogene surmised was) a *very* nice part of town. Oddly, it was connected (by means of a covered bridge behind a holly tree) to the overdressed house next door. Imogene wondered if they shared staff; why else build a passage between two homes?

Perhaps it was a werewolf thing.

Lady Maccon jumped off at the stoop with the ease of long practice. The front door was opened by an efficient-looking butler. She trotted up, waving at Imogene to follow.

Imogene climbed off her ride's fuzzy back. "Thank you very much for the lift, Major Channing."

The white wolf wagged his tail at her.

"You aren't coming in?"

He inclined his head to where Lord Maccon was already leading the rest of the pack away.

Lady Maccon said from the doorway, "They're off for a run. Be back in a bit."

Inside, the house was humming with activity. Imogene got a glimpse of what Woolsey Castle must have been like before the hive took it over. The walls were modestly bare and the furnishings very solid and rather sparse. A few of the receiving rooms were richly decorated in a tasteful masculine style, but there were no claw marks or scratches so far as she could see.

Lady Maccon led her upstairs. "You keep daylight hours, I understand?"

"Yes, ma'am."

"Genevieve said she found it easier in the country. Appalling idea, all that sunlight. We're night folk in this household, obviously. So, I'm afraid we will all be up and about while you sleep. I've a council meeting and Conall has his BUR duties to consider. The pack will return, make an obscene amount of noise, and then be off again. I'm sorry if they wake you."

She led Imogene to a lovely little guest room in the family section of the house.

"Oh, Lady Maccon, this is too much. I'm only a parlourmaid."

Lady Maccon frowned. "I thought you were Genevieve's assistant."

"Well, yes, now, or until recently. But before that, I was a maid."

Lady Maccon shrugged. "Well, this will do either way, won't it? You must be tired. Stop fussing and get some rest. We'll talk later when you've had a chance to orient yourself. I'll check in on you before I go to bed in the morning. Sound good?"

She certainly did like to manage things, Lady Maccon.

"Yes, ma'am."

"Good night, Imogene."

"Good night, ma'am."

Imogene spent a week in the London Pack house. She missed the noises of the lab, and the scent of vanilla, and the sidelong flash of hunger from Genevieve's eyes.

But London was an education. Not only because Lady Maccon gave her books to read to occupy her time. ("No, we don't have any poetry, dear, can't see the use in it, myself.") No one found her questions intrusive, so Imogene learned a great deal about how wolf packs functioned. The Maccons gave Imogene no duties, nor did they impose on her in any way. The rest of the pack and clavigers were polite but didn't know what to make of her. Fortunately, their lives were filled with reacting to the various quirks of Lady Maccon, thus they showed no surprise at Imogene's presence – considering it just one more quirk. They accepted her as they accepted all strange things that had come into their lives since their Alpha had married.

She met the Maccons' daughter, a cheerful child with her mother's forthright attitude and her father's eyes. No one explained her, and Imogene felt it rude to ask how such a creature could come into existence. She was well protected, spending most of her time next door with her guardian.

Only Major Channing made any kind of effort, and he seemed motivated by pity. He brought Imogene a paper packet of lemon sweets one evening, and roasted chestnuts a few nights later.

"Humans enjoy such things, I believe."

"You're too kind." Imogene had taken to rising before dawn so she could say hello before the pack went to bed.

"Well, poor little bite, you had to go and fall in love with that one."

Imogene wasn't going to deny it. She nibbled on a chestnut. "You know Madame Lefoux?"

"Tolerably. Alpha had me track her and Lady Maccon across Europe once, then we had to travel home together. She makes life difficult for herself, I think."

Imogene nodded, morose. "You're likely right."

"I usually am." Major Channing was nothing if not arrogant. Imogene didn't mind. She knew arrogance well. Even if he was not about to let her see the cause. His protective walls had been built up for far longer than hers.

And mine pretty much crumbled before one spectacular set of dimples. Well, fine, two sets of dimples. Imogene flinched. She didn't want to think about Genevieve naked right now.

"Any advice on how to manage her?" Imogene took another bite.

She and Major Channing had settled into a casual almost-sibling relationship in a very short space of time. In any other circumstances, such a quick camaraderie would have felt odd – he had the poshest accent of any man she'd ever met. A werewolf outranked her already, but this one must have started life amongst society's elite. But everything about her current situation was so surreal, Imogene accepted his brotherly friendship without worry. If before she'd been sleepwalking, now she was in a dream.

The werewolf shook himself. "As if I know anything about women. Nigh on a century and they still confuse me." He seemed to remember that he was supposed to be a cad. "Of course, I know a great deal about *one* aspect of women, should you ever wish to switch sides." He leered.

Imogene patted his cheek in a poor-old-wolf kind of way.

He went on, "But love? Bah."

"Very helpful, thank you."

"Have another chestnut."

At the end of the week, Imogene was summoned to tea with Lady Maccon. The mistress of the household was spectacularly dressed in a gown of dark green silk split down the bodice in a long V, and slit up the skirt from hem to waist, both slashes showing a quantity of expensive white lace. She'd clearly been visiting someone very important. Her bosoms were well contained, which came as a relief to Imogene.

"Sit down, dear, do. I'm terribly sorry that I've have taken so long to get around to your problems. But I could hardly spare the time, I've been *that* busy, and frankly, I think it a good idea to let the countess cool off. And Genevieve stew a little."

Imogene sat. She herself was in a new dress, Lady Maccon having insisted on supplying her with a whole new wardrobe. Imogene refused anything fancy, but the clavigers could be most insistent. Her gown was cream poplin with pink-and-green embroidered flowers about the skirt, a wide sash at the waist, and a full pleated bodice. There was a little muslin ruffle at the neckline (which was lower than anything she would've dared wear at the hive house). It had a robe-like overdress of pink to match. It was prettier than anything she'd ever owned.

Lady Maccon smiled. "I'm sure you're accustomed to my forthright ways by now."

Imogene thought Lady Maccon was being kind to herself. Unless by *forthright* she meant *blunt to the point of rudeness*. But she was also a gracious hostess.

Lady Maccon continued, "Genevieve is a dear friend. I wish to see her happy."

"As do I."

"Good. Very good. So, and not to be too direct, but do you love her?"

Imogene's odd, confusing dream, full of massive wolves and aggressive bosoms, came crashing down to reality. A reality in which she'd run away from Genevieve, left her alone in that horrible hive. A reality where she was torn between a vampire queen who wanted her dead and an inventor who wanted her, but not enough.

"It is impossible."

"My dear girl, didn't you know? *Impossible* is my specialty. Well?"

"Yes, yes, I do love her. Very much. But she is not interested. Not in the way that matters." The words tumbled out of her. It was nice to talk about it with someone who apparently didn't give two figs for the fact that both parties were female. "She is

wonderful and so much..." Just as abruptly,
Imogene's words dried up.

"So much *Genevieve*. Yes, I know. It can be
overwhelming, can't it? She's been waiting for you,
though, I think. A long time. You're a balance to her.
She's always needed someone to love and love wholly
with every part of herself. And you would not make
that difficult for her. I think the two of you, together,
will suit very well. It's a matter of convincing her, and
you, that you're the right woman for the job."

Imogene, despite herself, felt hope rise in her
breast. Everything seemed so practical and easy to
solve, when Lady Maccon was quizzing it. And to
have an ally was quite unexpected. (Well, an ally
besides Skoot. Skoot was always on her side.)

The woman rose and began to pace about. "It
seems to me that the most immediate problem of the
countess's ire could be solved by keeping you out of
the hive house at a sufficient distance from the
vampires. The countess can't leave the house at all,
and her tethered males can't go much beyond the
grounds. If we were to place you somewhat beyond
the lake – water is often an issue with tethers – that
would be extra protection. You could walk to work in
the potting shed during the day with no further fang
problems. I presume you can cook?"

"Well enough, but not for quality." *Is she going
to insist I camp in a field like a vagrant? Or put me to
work in a nearby manor house's kitchen?*

"You are my indenture. I'll increase your
remuneration for work in the lab. Genevieve and I will
determine the particulars. That way, you'll have

enough income to purchase food at a local market, or wherever it is that one obtains food in the country."

"We have a greengrocer's, ma'am, exactly like town."

"Do you indeed? How modern. Would that work?"

"Admirably. My salary is already sufficiently generous, thank you. But where would I live? The nearest village is too far to walk every day." *My village.* Imogene loathed the idea of returning home. To a life of hiding and being scared all the time. Never again. She'd rather risk her neck and stay with the hive.

"I've an idea about that too, but we must also solve the other matter."

"What other matter?"

"Genevieve herself. How to convince her that fool Angelique was a nasty flibbertigibbet nothing, and that you, my dear, are genuine?"

"I am?"

"Most definitely."

Imogene took a breath, found her courage, and confessed the greatest treasure of her heart. "I think she might love me back, if only a little."

"Oh, I think she might love you back a great deal. I've never seen her so focused on anyone. Back there at the hive, she never took her eyes off you. And she overreacted. Genevieve *only* overreacts for the people she loves. We've been in some pretty sticky situations together, she and I, and she was always cool as the proverbial cucumber until Angelique got killed and Quesnel got kidnapped."

So, she knew about that, did she?

"May I ask something quite impertinent?" The large nose beaked in Imogene's direction.

She'd been so helpful, Imogene felt compelled to say, "Of course, Lady Maccon."

"Oh, call me Alexia, do."

"Alexia."

"Have you two been intimate?'

Imogene blushed. "Only the once."

"Well, that should help."

"Should it?"

Alexia looked wise. "Yes, I think it generally does. People always say carnal relations complicate matters. I find it quite the opposite – simplifies everything down to its purest form. I take it things went well?"

That was a bit too intrusive, but then again, Alexia and Genevieve did flirt an awful lot. So Imogene said, "Wonderfully."

Alexia looked a tiny bit wistful. "Yes, I always imagined things would with Genevieve."

Imogene felt an odd combination of jealousy, pride, and superiority.

Lady Maccon, who seemed more a force of obtuse nature than anything else, didn't notice. "Not that I regret my choice, mind you. Conall's impossible but highly stimulating, and I've never felt anything lacking in the rough-and-tumble. It's only that I'm one of those people who, at the dinner table, wants to try *all the dishes*. You see my point?"

Imogene didn't.

Alexia didn't care, continuing blithely on with a,

"Too late now, of course."

"Um," said Imogene.

"Now, where was I? Oh, yes. I think you should get Genevieve soused."

"What!"

"Let me iron out the particulars of getting you back working together, *without vampires*, and you get her tipsy. Truth in the wine and all that rot. Although, in this case, love in the cognac. Genevieve adores a good cognac. I've got a bottle here. Use it wisely."

Imogene took the proffered bottle, which was likely worth more than all the new dresses in her wardrobe combined. She cradled it like a baby. It was really too much. The pack had already been overly generous. One of them, a charming young blighter named Biffy whom all the others seemed to regard with an unexpected degree of reverence, had taken her shopping *three* times. And once for nothing but hats!

"Oh, but—"

"I insist. Now, give me another few days to work things out, and I will see you settled in fine style. Speaking of which, I'll need Biffy for this. And possibly some of Akeldama's drones."

She stood, already charging towards the next step in her mysterious plan.

Imogene took that as a dismissal and, clutching her cognac, made her way out into the hall and up to her room.

Behind her, Lady Maccon yelled at the top of her lungs, "Biffy! Interiors are afoot! Oh, where is the boy? Biffy, I need you to *design* something beautiful!"

CHAPTER TEN

In Which We Solve All Equations

Lady Maccon's grand plan, as it turned out, was a massive gypsy caravan of some modern, technologically expansive design. She had it parked in the fields beyond the Woolsey lake. She'd apparently arranged everything with the hive, swinging her muhjah power about like a very big stick (or should one say *parasol*?). The pack dug it in and stabilized it in a pretty little meadow with silver birches around three sides and a view of the lake to the front. Lady Maccon, being practical, insisted on a vegetable garden, and the werewolves, being not as practical, thought flower boxes a wonderful idea.

The meadow was cheerful with the noises of birds. Bunnies appeared in the early morning, cotton tails twitching, although they fled as soon as they smelled wolf. Imogene noticed for the first time how little wildlife had been near the hive house. Vampires, she supposed, had a certain aura that prey animals would find oppressive. She understood the feeling entirely.

Biffy had decorated the caravan interior in fine style. It was quite spacious with a large bed, two small wardrobes, and a little pot-bellied stove. It even boasted a tiny desk-meets-dining-table in the kitchen area and a few shelves for Imogene's book collection. (Which only amounted to two, but Imogene had big dreams.)

Imogene loved it. The stove was perfect for both cooking and warmth, and there were Carcel lamps for light at night. A number of knobs and levers allowed most of the larger pieces of furniture to shift about as needed – so the bed might flip up, or the stove rotate away, or the table convert into a bench. All in all, it was more luxurious (and adaptive) than anything Imogene had ever occupied.

The night was full of quiet owl noises and the rustle of wind through the trees. The big bed felt empty, and Imogene couldn't help picturing Genevieve nestled next to her, but she slept soundly despite the lack.

The next day, Imogene returned to work in the potting shed.

Genevieve was clearly delighted to see her. Possibly because the laboratory was in utter chaos.

How has everything gotten so messy? I've only been gone a week!

"Oh, thank heavens you are back. I cannot find anything!" The inventor sounded casual, but her green eyes traced every part of Imogene's face.

Worryingly, Genevieve was looking even more

gaunt. *Has she eaten anything while I've been gone?*

"Are you all right, Imogene?"

"Lady Maccon has been very kind."

"Has she indeed? What does she want?"

Imogene leaped to Alexia's defense. "She has only your best interests at heart, I'm sure."

"Says she!" But there was no malice in it.

"She asked me to mention her new parasol order?"

"Yes, yes, I know. I have her specifications here somewhere. I suppose we should get started. I do owe her a massive favor."

"Oh, and she wanted me to remind you, you'll be seeing her soon."

"I will?"

"Sunday supper, next month? She wrote a note. Here it is." Imogene passed it over.

Genevieve cracked the seal and read it, hooting with laughter at the end. She handed it back to Imogene. "Go on. Read it yourself."

> *Genevieve,*
>
> *Don't be difficult about Sunday.*
> *You clearly aren't eating properly and I*
> *expect everything to be settled by then.*
> *Bring Imogene. The pack likes her. I like*
> *her. Don't be a noodle about this.*
>
> *Yours, etc.,*
> *Alexia*
>
> *P.S. You may buy me a replacement*
> *cognac.*

"What's this about cognac?" asked Genevieve.

Imogene put down the note, avoiding the question, and remarked, "She's kind of like an odd, loud, fierce fairy godmother, isn't she?" She wandered over to the waiting tea-tray and, lifting the lid, found a tempting plate of bacon and eggs.

"I'm starved. Come and join me, Genevieve, and I'll tell you what happened."

Imogene, of course, didn't tell her everything. But she did tell her all about the pack and what she'd learned.

"You cannot possibly be implying that you *like* Channing?"

Imogene nodded. Pleased to see Genevieve eat a whole plate of eggs and two rashers of bacon. *Excellent, the ploy worked.*

"We are talking about Major Channing Channing of the Chesterfield Channings?"

"Why, is there another one?"

"*Merde*. The very idea. Heaven forefend."

Imogene would not be moved. "He's sweet. He brought me chestnuts."

"What *has* the pack done to you?"

Imogene only smiled. "Would you like some more bacon?"

Genevieve began eating properly again. She put on a little weight. She was equally solicitous of Imogene's well-being. Sometimes overly so. No one from the hive bothered them, not even the gardeners. They both took great pains to break before dark so Imogene could walk back to her caravan safely.

Genevieve even kissed Imogene a few times.

Once on the top of her head, when she was bent over a schematic. Then again, a week after her return, right before Imogene left for the night. That kiss had been long and deep, pressing her up against the side of the door. Then the inventor had backed away with a muttered apology.

That week's separation, it turned out, had indeed worked wonders.

Ten days after her return, Imogene decided to try again in earnest.

"Would you like to see my caravan? It's very nice inside. Has all sorts of gadget-driven functionality – convertible table and a fold-away bed." She said this casually as they were winding down for the evening.

The inventor looked elated at the invitation and dropped the device she was disassembling with gratifying alacrity. She was usually not so quick to leave off her work.

Since Imogene's return, Genevieve had been dressing better than a potting shed really warranted. Each day, she seemed to choose a nicer waistcoat, even donning a cravat, as though she wished to make a good impression.

Imogene was suitably impressed and hoped she was the one who was meant to be. She imagined unwrapping the length of cravat and gliding it over Genevieve's body. She found herself fascinated by the way Genevieve's shoulders looked under her jacket, which she insisted on wearing every day when they took their afternoon walk about the garden.

Imogene had been thinking a lot about all of Genevieve's dimples.

That particular evening, Genevieve shrugged into a lovely grey morning coat and a top hat. She looked very fine indeed.

Imogene took the offered arm and they made their way across the garden to the lake. She remembered their first walk together. Her hand was steady now, not nervous or sweaty at all.

Genevieve Lefoux fit perfectly into Imogene's caravan. She explored all the gadgets and then sat comfortably at the little table. Her hat rested on a peg near the door, a peg that had confused Imogene. There were several of them, which she now realized were clearly meant for gentlemen's hats.

She began to understand why there were two wardrobes. Lady Maccon was very crafty indeed.

Imogene said, hopefully, "They built me a proper privy as well. Although, if I want to bathe, there's really only the lake."

"You can come back to the hive house for a proper bath, if you like. During the daytime, it wouldn't be difficult."

"I might take you up on that when it gets colder. Would you like a glass of cognac? Alexia gave it to me."

"Alexia, is it?"

"We've come to an understanding. I like her."

"It's rare, those who do. She seems to have done you proud with this caravan."

"Yes. Although I think perhaps Biffy had a hand in choosing and decorating it."

"Yes, looks like him. Only Biffy would remember hat pegs. Did you say something about cognac?"

Imogene went to get two small blue mugs, pouring a large measure into one and a lesser amount into the other.

Genevieve took the offered mug with a raised eyebrow. "Are you trying to get me drunk, Miss Hale?"

"Will it work?"

"Very likely. I promise not to put up much resistance." She leaned closer to Imogene, sipping the cognac, green eyes bright and intent.

"Changed your mind?" They were not talking about cognac. Imogene stroked the inventor's hand where it rested on the small table.

Genevieve turned it over instantly to lace their fingers together. "I realized something while you were away."

Imogene held her breath.

"That fountain I talked about? It's not as dry as I thought."

Imogene grinned. "Good. That's very good." Pride held her in check, although she wanted to lean forward and kiss the other woman, taste the cognac on her lips. Better than drinking it straight; it was horrible stuff. Burned all the way down.

"You're not pouncing on me. I thought you might pounce. Have I lost my chance with you, then?"

Imogene decided she had no pride and pounced.

The caravan, as it turned out, was sturdier than it looked. It hardly rocked at all.

What had been wonderful the first time around was extraordinary the second. Genevieve was much less tentative. She seemed determined to leave no part of Imogene's body unexplored.

Imogene, of course, felt the same.

They took their time, less frantic than that first night. Imogene no longer feared that Genevieve might flee at the slightest opportunity. And Genevieve was intent on proving her interest genuine in every way possible. Imogene was delighted to have her try. It was a glorious thing, to be wooed.

It was an exercise in hedonism. Particularly when Genevieve poured a tiny measure of cognac into Imogene's belly button and licked it out. Then kept licking lower, her mouth cool from the alcohol, her tongue teasing.

Those callused fingers could do wicked things to Imogene's body – firm and sure when required, gentle and stroking the rest of the time. Imogene crested and panted and crested again – arching and writhing and whimpering under her touch. She was desperate to touch in return, to sink her teeth (only a little) into Genevieve's white thigh (she yelped, which was wonderful) and to see her writhe in turn.

Eventually, they were both mere puddles of joy.

Imogene remembered the analogy then, and wondered if she were fountain enough for the both of them. If she could give enough love for the little drops that she would get in return.

She decided she was. That if this was all they had, an idyllic evening on occasion, it would be enough. It was more than she'd ever hoped for, after all.

"I have missed you, *choupinette*." Genevieve was draped partly over her, naked and satiated. She buried her face in Imogene's hair.

Imogene curled a hand over Genevieve's neck, feeling the slight bumps that formed the octopus tattoo, then threading her fingers up though the short curls above. She inhaled vanilla and hope. "Can't handle the equations without me, hum?"

"Yes. Well, no, but that's not what I meant. I missed *you*. I missed the way you move about the lab. The curve of your cheek when you rest your chin on your hand to think. The weight of your hair. The way you stick the tip of your tongue out when you are concentrating really hard."

"I do not!"

"Oh, yes, you do. It is adorable. You also mouth words when you are reading. I want to kiss you so badly when you do that."

"You've my permission to do so from here on out. Although try not to disturb me too much." She was being coy. "I do love reading. It's such a joy."

Genevieve stilled against her.

Imogene stopped stroking her neck. *So, here the rejection comes this time.* She took a deep breath, preparing herself.

Imogene might have predicted many things, but she was not prepared for pleading in her inventor's voice.

"May I come live here, with you?"

"Yes," said Imogene on an exhalation. She didn't even have to think about it. Her skin prickled. "It's made for both of us."

"Good. I shall have to barter a longer indenture so they let me move out of the hive. Could be as much as ten additional years."

"I'll stay with you as long as is necessary." *I'll stay with you forever.*

Genevieve ran a hand up and down Imogene's side. It only tickled a little. "I won't mind as much, being here."

Imogene tried to keep the mood light. "And I shall have access to all your books."

Genevieve sat back and looked around the caravan's interior. "We'll have to store some of them in the potting shed not quite enough shelf space here." Then, all of a sudden, she grinned.

Imogene sat up at that, driven to nuzzle in against the dimples. Self-consciously, she whispered, "I kept one of my parlourmaid's dresses and a duster."

"To wear for me?"

"I thought you might like—"

A kiss fairly scalded her mouth at that. "Oh, I like."

A pause while they both gathered their wits about them. Imogene delighted in the effectiveness of the mere mention of that dress.

Genevieve drew her in close, petting her, swirling her thumb over Imogene's hipbone. "I speak four languages, you know. French, German, English, and Latin."

Imogene blinked at the change of subject. "I didn't know about the Latin."

"I shall teach you to read in all of them."

Imogene collapsed against her in delight, twisting them around so that Genevieve was on her back and Imogene sprawled atop her. She peppered her inventor with tiny kisses until, out of breath, she finally stopped.

Genevieve was giggling. Actually giggling.

Imogene kissed her deeply on the mouth, tongue and everything – glorying in the fact that this roughened Genevieve's breathing, and the restless way she shifted beneath her.

Imogene stopped long enough to say, "I should like to learn French first, please."

"*Je t'aime*," said Genevieve.

"What does that mean?" Imogene's eyes were wide, hoping for something quite naughty, perhaps a suggestion or a position?

"I love you," said Genevieve.

Imogene burst into tears.

Genevieve tried to calm her with cognac.

Then with a long and thorough embrace.

Then she told her all the truths of her heart, now filled to bursting. That she'd realized Imogene was different and wouldn't betray her. That they might be there together, and that they might be loved, both of them worthy of it.

She'd even let Skoot come and visit them in the lab more often.

When none of these tactics worked on Imogene's (joyful) histrionics, the inventor gave her an equation to solve.

Imogene solved it, of course. For x, as it turned out, equaled two.

GLOSSARY OF TERMS

Aetherogram: The message transmitted by an aethographor. The aethographor is a wireless communication apparatus that does not suffer from electromagnetic disruption like the telegraph (which was abandoned as a failure). Two machines with matching valves (properly termed *crystalline valve frequensors*) can transmit messages through the aether to each other.

BUR: The Bureau of Unnatural Registry, part of the British government. It has oversight of werewolves, vampires, ghosts, preternaturals, and metanaturals within the British Empire. The organization is headquartered in London, and Conall Maccon, Alpha for the Woolsey/London werewolf pack, is head of the London BUR office and Chief Sundowner (licensed killer).

Claviger: Clavigers act as servants and companions to werewolves, and are paid for their services with the possibility of becoming werewolves themselves. Their duties include looking after out-of-control werewolves on and around the full moon, and taking care of any business the pack has that needs to be conducted during daylight hours.

Drone: A drone acts as a vampire's companion, servant, caretaker, and willing food source (blood). There can also be a sexual component to the relationship. Drones receive payment for their services in the possibility of becoming vampires themselves.

Hive: A hive is a group of vampires and their particular residence. A hive is always ruled by a vampire queen, who cannot leave the hive house and relies on the vampires that belong to her hive and their drones to represent her in the outside world.

Indenture: An indentured servant or worker owes their time and labor to the person or institution holding their indenture for a prescribed amount of time. In exchange, they are paid a salary and trained in a certain skill set. In some cases, the education comes first, then once educated, the skilled laborer is indentured to pay back the cost of that education.

Muhjah: The third member of the Shadow Council; a preternatural. This advisor to Queen Victoria is meant to break the stalemate between the potentate (vampire) and the dewan (werewolf). He or she represents the voice of the modern age, as opposed to the other two older, set-in-their-ways advisors.

Sootie: Children who work in the boiler rooms of airships, shoveling coal.

Confused by any other terms used in this story? Try the Gail Carriger wikia.

AUTHOR'S NOTE

Thank you so much for picking up *Romancing the Inventor*. If you enjoyed it, or if you would like to read more about any of my characters, please say so in a review. I'm grateful for the time you take to do so.

I have a silly gossipy newsletter called the Monthly Chirrup. I promise: no spam, no fowl. (Well, maybe a little fowl and the occasional giveaway.) Join it on my website.

gailcarriger.com

ABOUT THE WRITERBEAST

New York Times bestselling author Gail Carriger writes to cope with being raised in obscurity by an expatriate Brit and an incurable curmudgeon. She escaped small-town life and inadvertently acquired several degrees in higher learning, a fondness for cephalopods, and a chronic tea habit. She then traveled the historic cities of Europe, subsisting entirely on biscuits secreted in her handbag. She resides in the Colonies, surrounded by fantastic shoes, where she insists on tea imported from London.

Made in USA - Crawfordsville, IN
28750_9781944751074
04.11.2020 1535